M

TIMEWALKER CHRONICLES BOOK 1: RED NIGHT

MICHELE CALLAHAN

Timewalker Chronicles, Book 1:

RED NIGHT

by Michele Callahan

Donna –
Hope you enjoy the
story! Pleasure meeting you.
Michele Callahan

TIMEWALKER CHRONICLES BOOK 1: RED NIGHT

Ω
RED NIGHT

Deception…
Luke Lawson is walking into a trap. Brilliant, dedicated, and haunted by strange visions, he guards his mistake well, determined to eliminate anyone or anything that threatens to unleash his creation upon the world. But his enemy is vicious, smart, and oh-so-patient. He has been watching…waiting to strike.

Duty…
Alexa wants no part of her family's ancient bargain with the Archiver, nor does she want the 'gift' that makes her something more than human. But should she refuse the call for help, six billion people will die from a horrible bio-agent known as the Red Death. Sent back through time to prevent the global disaster. She has three days to track down the man responsible and eliminate the danger.

Destiny…
Alexa begins her hunt. However, once she meets Luke, her desire to save him becomes stronger than the cold logic demanding she kill him. The viral cultures are missing, Luke's superiors are keeping deadly secrets, and the clock is ticking. Humanity's very survival depends on them discovering the true enemy before it's too late. Secrecy. Sedition. Seduction. They are playing a deadly game…and they can't afford to lose.

TIMEWALKER CHRONICLES BOOK 1: RED NIGHT

I dedicate this story to the women who have made my life so much more than a series of dates on a calendar. What fun would life be without friends?

Mom and Grandma Opal (I miss you both so much!)
Cyndi F, Cyndi O, Cindy W, Debbie, Indra, Jan, Janon, Jennifer, Kally, Kandi, Karen, and my dear sisters Rebecca and Trena. I love you all. Thanks for everything!

TIMEWALKER CHRONICLES BOOK 1: RED NIGHT

Ω
Prologue

Timewalker: *Alexa, Seventeenth Daughter of Aryssa*
Mission: *Present Day, Earth - Destroy the Red Death*
Talent: *Invisibility*

Despite years of warnings, Alexa was not prepared for the freezing shock of her journey to Earth. She wanted to scream in agony, but she had no air to breathe in this in-between dimension. Her mother had explained the frigid reality of the time strands, how her naked flesh would feel as if it were being systematically stripped to her bones by endless shards of splintering ice. This one-way trip to the past would last less than a minute. One minute in her own personal Purgatory, and her sins had been many. So, she gritted her teeth and waited. Waited for the agony to subside. Waited for the nirvana of soft green grass brushing at her skin like a thousand tickling fingertips.

Her mother had been Taken, and her mother before her, and so on, since the Archivers had begun recording the Chronicles Of Time. Death or Service. That had been her ancestor's choice nearly four hundred years ago, and the eldest daughter in each generation now owed the Archiver a life. The family gift -- invisibility -- had been handed down from mother to daughter for seventeen generations. Her heritage swelled her head and chest with pride. But the unrelenting grip of her ancestry also squeezed her with arduous pressure, demanding she not fail. She did not want to be the first of her line to bring her name dishonor. However, a far heavier burden threatened to pull her into the suffocating quicksand of fear. Billions of lives were at stake. Billions.

She would not fail. She was ready. Her mother had ensured that, taught her how to use her gift to cloak her presence, prepared her for the call of the Archiver and the freezing strands. The Taken were never called upon to ride the strands of time unless the assignment was of catastrophic importance. There was no such thing as an easy task. She had also warned her daughter not to fall victim to the pounding of the blood, the passion of her Gift, until it was safe to do so. The distraction would endanger the strand of time she must now, and forever after, walk upon.

Forever. In a strange world.

Alone.

Panic rose in a crescendo to choke her. Then, as quickly as her roller coaster ride through this icy hell began, it was over. Precious air flooded her starving lungs with heat. She lay semi-conscious on the soft ground and tried to get her bearings as a torrent of warm rain crashed down upon her. A single tear escaped and mingled with the rain on her face. Reality squeezed her heart so tightly she feared it would stop beating. She had arrived, unscathed. There was no going back.

Earth, Midnight, May 6, 2013. Unless the Archiver had erred.

Heaven help her then. Heaven help the world.

Ω

Chapter One

Never once, in all the years of her rebellious youth, had she ever been a thief. How ironic that now, when the fate of this world hung in the balance, everything she had was contraband. She leaned back into the taxi's sticky plastic seat and hoped the crisp white cotton Capri pants and shirt wouldn't be ruined by the filth. A twenty-dollar bill burned in her pocket to pay the cabbie. Alexa sunk her teeth into a huge red apple and hoped the fruit would provide enough energy to keep her going for a few hours. Doom Central was calling her name.

Alexa laughed out loud at her own joke and ignored the cab driver's questioning glance. The overworked cabbie should be used to seeing all sorts of odd things in a city the size of San Antonio. But even here, she knew she was unique. Her waist-length hair was braided and so pale it gleamed silver. Her eyes flashed a vivid blue in a heart-shaped face. Father had always said she was sixty-two inches of trouble wrapped up in a deceptively innocent looking package. The thought made her want to laugh. And cry.

Too soon the cab driver dropped her off at her destination, one of a handful of Biosafety Level 4 laboratories in the country. The lucky place which, in three days time, would be the epicenter of the end of the world. Earth 8 had died a slow and painful death. It took just under five years from the first diagnosed case of "Red Death" for ninety-five percent of the world's population to be wiped out. And it all started here. No-Where-Ville, Texas. A party like any other…a night colored red with blood.

Yes. She had three more days to track down the two men in charge, erase every piece of data related to the virus, and break into that lab and kill every single cell of "Mutation-6 of Ebola" in existence. M-6 they called it, until it escaped. Then it became the "Red Death", named for the hemorrhagic nature of the victim's death. They should have called it, "stupid-what-the-hell-were-we-thinking?"

"Men." The car stopped. Alexa slid out of the back seat of the cab, ignored the driver's mumbling, and handed him the twenty through his open window with a bright smile pasted on her full pink lips. "Always think they can beat Mother Nature."

Alexa turned away from the cab. The driver took off mumbling about the faults of crazy women. When she was sure he was gone, she quickly jogged to within sight of the eight hundred twenty-one acre complex.

It was still early. She stopped to lean against the fence and calm her mind. It took tremendous energy to draw the light to her body and redirect it, rendering herself invisible. Cloaking, her mother called it. The semi-dark of pre-dawn would help her avoid unwanted notice. Once she was forced to cloak her presence, she wouldn't be able to sustain the illusion for more than a couple of hours without a break. And then she'd be so hungry, she'd probably kill for a sandwich.

She patted the protein bar and mozzarella cheese stick in her pants pocket for courage and mumbled to herself, "Such is the glamorous life of the Timewalker."

The building employees changed shifts at 8:00 a.m. A quick glance at her stolen Tinkerbelle watch told her she had fifteen minutes. Already, parking lot activity was picking up. Time to move in.

Alexa closed her eyes and stilled the chaos of her mind, called upon the quiet, watchful awareness within herself that allowed her to use her gift. She envisioned herself a small white crystal in a river of light, and pushed the rays out and around her until it flowed like water over a small rock. Many times she'd watched her mother, practiced, and studied the effect in a mirror. It was like looking at something you thought was there, but could never quite see. Bright light made it harder to hide the soft edges of the effect. It wasn't perfect, but no one could see her unless they knew what to look for.

Luckily for her, no one would be looking. Besides, no one could be truly awake at this ungodly hour. She needed at least two cups of coffee to form a coherent thought before noon. This morning she'd had five.

Silent as a shadow, she crept up to the double glass doors at the entrance and scouted the parking lot for someone she could follow in. Security demanded an access card to get in the front door. She must follow someone into the building, and find one of the two men she knew would have the highest level clearance, and direct access to the viral cultures. Trent Georges or Luke Lawson. Once she spotted either of them, she'd stick to him like a parasite would lunch, steal his badge, and start World War III against the bugs. Getting caught would mean disaster, so she'd have to be extremely careful.

Break into the lab, destroy every single deadly virus, erase all computer files and research materials, track down and follow two men to their homes, evaluate them as threats, kill them if necessary, and eliminate any study material they kept at home. Crush flash drives. Hack into their e-mail. A sigh escaped before she could stop it. Three days suddenly didn't feel like very long at all. And she'd already been in this world for several hours.

A loud, and obnoxiously unconcerned whistle sang through the air, freezing her in place. A quick chorus of 'Good mornings' followed. Alexa turned to see who was making all the commotion and nearly jumped at her good fortune.

Target Number One was heading right for the front doors.

Luke Lawson was the microbiologist in charge of the Ebola studies. He answered to only one man, Trent Georges, head of the foundation. God had just given her a gift, wrapped up in a tall, sexy package, and she meant to follow him.

Alexa moved quickly, darted right in behind him, and glued herself to his back. She got so close to his muscular frame that his navy blazer sleeves lightly brushed against her breasts a time or two, sending tingles through her entire body.

Great. Hormone overload was just what she needed right now. Did her mother always have to be right?

Four people on an elevator shouldn't seem like too many, but then she'd never been trying to hide in plain sight. Mr. Chatterbox wouldn't shut-up with the morning cheer either. Sandwiched between Luke and two women, she flinched in preparation for flight at their every twitch. Stuck on an elevator, she had nowhere to run. No, she didn't feel overly cheerful. All this happiness was going to give her a headache.

At least the other two women on the elevator weren't responding in kind. They seemed like much more reasonable people. Or, maybe Mr. Lawson had caffeine intravenously every morning. She snorted at the thought.

Luke stiffened, then turned to stare right down at her with chocolate brown eyes. Or rather, right *through* her.

She didn't dare move. A shiver threatened to explode from her body. Suppressing it forced goose bumps to jump out on her arms. Frozen in place like a panicked rabbit, Alexa held her breath, then retreated, and willed her body to shrink back into the unforgiving elevator wall. She prayed he wouldn't see her. After a moment, he frowned and turned back around to stare at the glowing numbers as they changed above the elevator doors. Without his chatter, all the air seemed to have left the elevator. What was left was too thick to breathe.

Nerves. Damn. The air escaped from her lungs in a slow controlled hiss when he stepped off the elevator. Scurrying after him, she dodged people in the hallways as she followed him to his office. Slumped against the wall, she waited for his door to close behind him. Good fortune was smiling upon her yet again. Directly across from his office was another door with the name of Mr. Red Death himself, Trent Georges.

She cupped her hands above her eyes and peered through the glass.

Empty.

A good ten minutes passed while she waited for the hallway to clear out. Someone would probably notice a door opening and closing by itself. Finally, after she'd stood there worrying about the entire mess long enough for sweat to pool and run down her cleavage, she managed to slip inside Trent's office.

Now she was really grumpy. She hated sweat.

All she needed was ten minutes. She hoped. His computer was state of the art. Not that it mattered. It only took her a few minutes to reboot and scramble his hard drive beyond repair. His notebooks and papers were next. There just happened to be a shredder in his office. Rolling her eyes, she wondered just what that was for. Trent was going to annihilate the whole world and he was probably worried about his checking account.

She glanced at Tinkerbelle again. Ten minutes. One third of her mission for the day accomplished. Not bad. But she was getting tired. And hungry. Very, very hungry.

Hungry, tired, doomed to sneak around like this for another couple of hours, and, last but not least, her chest still tingled. Now, this whole libido thing was just going to be a pain in the neck. Never before had desire overwhelmed her, threatened her ability to think. Not like this. Every heartbeat sent blood pounding through parts of her body she didn't have time to think about; and all because she'd walked the strands.

Her mother had tried to warn her of how years of sexual desire would exponentially explode after she reached her destination. Holy hell. Mom could have tried a little harder to convince her. Oh, well. She never was much for listening, anyway. And she sure as hell had never liked being told what to do. That's why she'd waited so long to answer her Archiver's call. The Archiver owned her. Had owned all the women of her line since time began. Something inside her really wanted to piss him off for that. For forcing her to leave everyone she loved, her parents, her eight brothers, her life. And for making the task so important that she wouldn't refuse the call.

Sometimes being honorable was hell. She hated the Archiver for giving her the choice. Petty? Sure. But she just couldn't help herself. She'd ignored him, hoping he would forget about her. Of course, her plan had failed. The Archiver operated outside the realm of normal time. Another ten years in her life would've made no difference to him. May, 2017 wasn't going anywhere. Disaster had already struck once. She was just here to try to prevent it from happening again, from becoming a permanent apocalypse. Her job was to change the past. Change the future, and not just for this planet. The ripple effect of the Red Death had caused more accumulative damage elsewhere. Parallel dimensions. It was one hell of a mess. And he'd sent her.

"Fool." Obviously he believed in her and her heritage. She wished with all her heart that she shared that faith.

Alexa listened to the muffled voices reverberating through the hallway for a moment before easing the office door open a couple of inches. Immediately Mr. Cheerful's voice nearly knocked her back inside the room.

"Are you insane, Trent?"

Yelling. High volume. Yes. Absolutely perfect. Luke Lawson's good mood seemed to have evaporated. A happy smirk slipped into place on her face. She couldn't help it. No one could maintain that much good cheer for long. It just wasn't possible. But even as the thought crossed her mind, she wondered what had happened to sour the morning for him.

"Look, Luke. If we don't take this to the next level, someone else will."

Alexa peeked around the edge of the door. A rather large man's back half protruded from the open doorway of Luke's office. She seized the opportunity and slipped out into the hallway while no one was looking. The big guy started talking again.

"We're on to something big here. We'll get millions in grants. If we don't start animal testing this vaccine, we're going to miss the boat. And then, when some freak attacks us with this shit, it'll wipe us all out."

Alexa slid across the hallway to get a look at the man's face. He had light blond hair, cut short and balding into deep widow's peaks. Alcohol had added a deep reddish flush to his cheeks and nose that contrasted starkly with otherwise pale skin. His eyes bulged from his head like an insect's, or like a bloated fish that had been lying too long in the sun. Black slacks hugged his oversized rear-end a little too tightly and her foot was within easy striking distance of his family jewels. She gritted her teeth and held herself in check. All Alexa really, really wanted was to kick him in the nuts.

Trent Georges himself was within striking distance, sounding like the fool history had proven him.

"No. Number six is the most virulent. The worst of the bunch. I can't believe I let you talk me into playing around with the damn thing in the first place." Alexa managed a quick glance around Trent. Luke was advancing on his cohort. Anger twisted his face, but his voice was deadly calm. "If you start testing on animals, you're exposing too many people. The vaccine hasn't been tested. You can't be serious."

Trent's voice could've been used to scold a two year old. "They'll be in quarantine. It'll be fine." Trent crossed his arms over his chest. "I submitted the project for approval months ago. Got it back last week. Donovan is getting the lab set up. You start Wednesday, or you resign. This is my project, Luke."

"Don't tell me. Richards signed off on it for you." Luke shook his head in disgust. "I don't care what that idiot in Washington approved. I won't do this, Trent."

"Don't be hasty." Trent backed into the hallway. "Go home. Think it over. This is a huge project. You'd be in charge. Frankly, Luke, you're the idiot if you pass this up."

Alexa dashed into Luke's office seconds before he slammed the door closed on Trent's retreating back. She made herself as small as possible in one corner and watched Luke slump down into the high back chair behind his desk. "Damn it. He doesn't even have the balls to work in the Hot Zone himself." Luke ran his hand through his hair, then his fingers pushed into his chest, like he was suffering a muscle twinge there. "He doesn't know what he's starting."

Thirty minutes later, obvious agitation quickened his steps as he paced his office. Back and forth. Back and forth. Desk to door. Door to desk. His nerves were waking hers up, feeding them more adrenaline for breakfast. Not good. Maybe if she could get to his computer, she could quietly get this part of the job done while he wasted time waltzing around his little playpen. And maybe she could stop staring at his tight buns in those khakis.

Yeah. Right. No chance in hell of that happening.

She edged closer to his heavy mahogany desk and the clutter splattered across its shining surface. Most likely, he would notice if she started tapping on his keyboard, but maybe she could get an idea of what he had around just by looking. What she really hoped was that her pulse would stop pounding in her ears.

Trent Georges had disgusted her. So why would his partner in crime turn her on? According to the history she'd been given, he was equally responsible for the outbreak. Just as many souls hung over his head. So, why didn't she feel their oppressive weight destroying the attraction when it came to him?

The only possibility appalled her. Destiny. Fate. The meddling of the Archiver with her life. And his. A silent "No" fell from her lips. Her jaw dropped at the realization and she couldn't tear her gaze from his muscular frame. Luke Lawson had wavy chestnut hair, just long enough to bury her hands in and sigh as its softness whispered over her skin. Chocolate brown eyes that would melt her on the spot if he'd actually been looking at her. Broad shoulders. Full soft lips. And his hands. Heaven help her. Every inch of her body begged to be worshipped by those incredible hands.

This can't be happening. She remembered her mother's throaty laugh when she'd boldly declared The Prize to be a joke. Alexa refused to believe the Archiver had the power to choose a mate for her before she'd even been born. Her mother had been happy to let the matter drop after a sly, "We'll see, daughter."

The Prize. The perfect man for her. A gift given in return for sacrificing her life to save others. A man genetically manipulated to be compatible with her DNA. A man who would sire the perfect daughter. A little girl who would be the next of her line to be Taken. A man who would boil her blood and be the ideal companion for her, for the rest of her life here on Earth 8. He was chosen by the wisest beings in existence, beings chosen by God Himself to protect all the planets, and the races on them, from themselves.

And her man whistled, at six o'clock in the morning.

Her man was responsible for the end of the world.

Luke was still crisscrossing his office like an enraged army ant rebuilding his fallen fortress. And he was all hers. If she could keep them both alive long enough to claim him.

Ω

Chapter Two

They must've made a mistake this time at the big meddlers' meeting. The Archiver who summoned her ordered her to do whatever was necessary to prevent the outbreak. That included eliminating the scientists responsible. Luke couldn't be hers. She was supposed to kill him. If she didn't, M-6 would. He was the third victim of the Red Death.

Even as she flirted with the thought, she knew there was no mistake. The cabbie, Trent, and all the men in the small army of staff that worked in this complex had failed to draw her attention. Nope. The only man she wanted was him. The whistler.

There was always the chance he'd be reasonable. How cruel a fate to be forced to kill her mate. Or anyone else for that matter. She wasn't at all sure she could do it. Hopefully, she wouldn't have to find out.

The urge to unmask her presence and tell him everything was nearly impossible to resist. If he were her true match, he would have to respond to her. To believe her. But what if he didn't? Could she risk billions of lives on a theory inspired by a hormonal surge? No.

Frustration built until it was gnawing a hole in her stomach two hours later. She couldn't allow Luke to get out of sight, so he'd led her on a merry chase around the complex. To the lab. Back to his office. More pacing. Conference room for a meeting where a bunch of stiffs argued over details that wouldn't matter in a week if the Red Death struck. Back to his office. Even more pacing. And mumbling. And cursing. She wanted to slap him upside the head and tell him to get on with it. He needed to go home so she could destroy any files he had there. He needed to get her inside the lab so she could wipe out all the bugs. And what was he doing? Sitting at his desk for the last half hour, working. There was nowhere she could hide in his

Spartan office and relax for a minute. Two chairs, one huge wall-to-wall bookcase stuffed to overflowing, and his desk occupied the small room. That was it. The plain tile floor didn't look comfortable, and the hallway was no better. No rest for the wicked. Problem was, she couldn't keep this up much longer, especially without food. She'd been cloaking herself for longer than she would've believed possible.

A slight tremor vibrated through the waves of light she could see cascading around her and she hoped he couldn't see her. The struggle to remain hidden drained her energy, and would soon force her to act in reckless desperation. Exhaustion made her hands shake and her right eyelid periodically twitch. All she really wanted was to devour several pounds of chocolate, then lie down and sleep for a week.

Fat chance of that happening.

But at least he wasn't whistling.

Surprisingly, she missed the sound. As obnoxious as she'd first thought his habit, the noise had calmed her nerves, just a bit. Oh, well. She'd wanted him to stop, and now he had. No sense whining about it.

Alexa sat in the brown leather chair across from his desk and studied him. Luke was scowling intently at his laptop computer. No matter how hard she tried to remember to control herself, her foot rebelled and periodically tapped the floor, betraying her irritation. His concentration was so complete he didn't hear it.

Enough! Time to get this fool out of here before she collapsed.

She sprang out of the chair and pulled the power cord out of his laptop. He frowned but didn't stop working.

As quietly as possible, she glided around his desk to check the computer screen. Battery back-up. Hell.

Resisting the temptation to touch him, she arched one arm around his broad shoulder and pushed in the power button. A delicious mix of coffee and aftershave lotion invaded her lungs, made her want to…

"What the…" Luke reached around, plugged the computer back in, and started to reboot. Stubborn man. An ornery giggle nearly escaped before she could swallow it down. This could get interesting.

He rebooted the computer. She crashed it. They went through the dance again. She knocked over his coffee when his arm got close to it. Journals and papers flipped onto the floor. She loosened all the adjustment knobs on his brown leather chair when he bent to retrieve them, so he was simultaneously dropped several inches and flipped back into a reclined position when he sat back down. Leaning in close to smell him again, she blew in his ear. The line of his tall frame beckoned her and she and imagined herself on his lap. Now, that situation had definite possibilities.

Luke got up, fixed his chair, sat down, and stared, dumbfounded, at his computer screen again. "All right. Enough." With an impatient shove, he closed the laptop and slammed it into its case. He grabbed a couple of periodicals off his desk and headed for the door.

Alexa would have jumped for joy, but she barely had the energy to keep up as his much-longer legs ate up the distance between the building and his black vehicle. The door said Cherokee, and for a fleeting instant she wondered if the Nation of United Tribes had started producing vehicles. This world was so like her own, and so not home.

She waited until he had the driver's door open to knock the magazines out of his hand. While he retrieved them, she crawled over the front seats and into the back. The moment the engine came to life she curled into a ball, prayed he wouldn't find her, and allowed exhaustion to overcome her.

When she awoke, she knew two things. It was dark. And she needed food. Her hunger went beyond the normal twinge of the stomach. The searing hunger pangs spread to her entire body, made every muscle quiver. She crawled into the back seat and looked around. She was in a garage. There was enough room for another vehicle, but parked there instead was a motorcycle with the words "Harley Davidson" on its side and several different styles of bicycles. A row of small windows stretched across the large door. Beyond them night had fallen.

A quick glance at Tinkerbelle's green glowing dial assured her the day was gone. Ten o'clock. Time was racing. The Red Death would soon be waving the final flag.

There was a single door she prayed led into his house. She grasped the door handle and breathed a sigh of relief when it turned easily in her hand. "Ready or not, here I come."

He was still awake. A light was on and background noise came from the other side of the house. She didn't care. All she cared about was food. If she didn't eat soon, the whole world could self-destruct and she wouldn't even notice. Her mother had always laughed at times like this, when she'd nearly gone mad with hunger after practicing her cloaking. Dad had accused her of being unreasonable and grumpy. Well, yeah. So, what? A girl couldn't save the world on an empty stomach. But it wasn't just her stomach that screamed for food. Her entire body felt hollow, like someone had sucked the marrow from her bones while she slept.

One more tiny problem. She didn't have enough energy left to hide her presence. The floor dipped and spun under her tennis shoes. Her stomach rolled and threatened the plush green carpeting in the hallway with a nasty deposit. "Damn." The whispered curse flew from her lips before she thought to stop it.

Leaning heavily against the wall, she felt her way down the dark hallway. The flickering of his television lights allowed her to find the kitchen.

The kitchen was separated from the other room by a row of cabinets on the floor and a chest high tile countertop bar and eating area. If she crouched below the bar level she wouldn't be seen. She was nearly too hungry to care. As quietly as possible, she eased open several cabinet doors until she found something edible. She examined the blue liquid in an unopened bottle that said "Gatorade". After a quick glance at the label, she decided it wouldn't kill her, and promptly drained it dry.

Her entire body sighed in relief as the sugar rush surged through her bloodstream. The stainless steel refrigerator door beckoned her from where she sat slumped on the cold tile floor. She needed more. What were the chances of him having a large turkey on wheat waiting for her, heavy on the mayo? Slim to none was her guess. But she was beyond being picky.

Luke was moving around in the other room. She heard a door open and close. Her eyelids drifted closed and she leaned her head against the oak cabinet door. How could she pull this off? How would she tell a complete stranger his bug was going to wipe out the planet? How would she convince him to destroy his life's work?

A quick peek up over the edge of the counter assured her that he hadn't moved in her direction, so she sank back onto the tile floor. Luke Lawson seemed like a decent man. He'd held his own against Trent. He'd been courteous to all of his staff during meetings when she was sure he would've been just as happy strangling some of them. What was going on inside his head? Would he think she was insane and call the police? Kick her out on her ear?

It didn't matter; she had to find a way to make him believe her. Without help, she couldn't get into the lab. She was no magician or electrical whiz. She wasn't a spy or even a very good sneak. Nope, she was just a normal everyday girl who happened to be able to be invisible once in a while. But you didn't need to be seen to be infected by a virus.

As much as she hated to admit the truth, she needed him, needed his help. She had to trust him. Unfortunately, thinking about it and doing it were two very different things.

* * *

Luke couldn't believe this day from hell. First, Trent came to him with a crazy scheme for a new strain and animal testing on the Ebola mutation. No one else in the project meeting had any objections to Trent's insanity. And, last but not least, he was sure he'd been followed all day. By an angel.

He'd finally done it, lost his mind. Willingly given himself to the insanity of her until he realized he was looking over his shoulder and actually hoping to catch another glimpse of silver hair. His angel had the fair face of an innocent young woman, but the haunted blue eyes of a woman who knew too much. His. The woman he'd dreamt about nearly every night since he was sixteen years old. The woman who'd marked him as her own when he was still just a boy.

On the night of his sixteenth birthday a strange man in a white robe had led him to her in a dream. In truth, he'd never believed it was real. But he'd never been able to stop thinking about her either. And in his dreams? No sane man would admit to the things he'd seen in his dreams.

Never before had his visions invaded the waking hours. Today, all day long, he'd caught glimpses of her flickering in and out, an illusion that stalked him. That's what he'd believed anyway. He'd even hung around work longer, hoping to see more of her, until a couple of books had fallen from his bookcase. His computer had gone crazy. And, he swore he'd heard a feminine voice whispering in his ear to go home. A voice that made his spine tingle and his pulse leap. Not good.

He'd given in and gone home. Just as he'd feared, she vanished. He was thirty-two years old. Too old to believe in nonsense.

He'd spent the evening in his study, on the telephone. Trent wasn't the only one with contacts in the Army's Biological Defense Program and the NIH. Luke hadn't worked very hard to convince the colonel the study was too dangerous. Especially once he read through the colonel's copy of Trent's M-6 report. Half of it, lies. Trent was obviously willing to do anything for a few million in grant money. Including risk the lives of everyone in the Hot Zone, a place Trent never entered unless he absolutely had to. The jackass always preferred someone else take the risks.

Luke chuckled to himself. He'd never liked Trent. Luckily, Trent had a few too many enemies in the Army. They'd been looking for an excuse to kick him off the project and transfer him out of BL4. Luke had happily supplied one. Day after tomorrow, more importantly, the day after their annual fundraiser, Trent was going to be in for one hell of a shock. The whole mutant project was going down. Every culture was to be destroyed. Luke was looking forward to doing the honors. He wished the colonel would let him do it tomorrow, but Trent was too good at schmoozing the moneymen. No one wanted to fire him until after he'd brought in the cash.

Luke leaned back in his brown leather sofa and propped his feet up on the mahogany coffee table. He'd won, beaten the slimeball at his own game. Tonight, he was going to sleep like a baby.

Shuffling? *Was that his refrigerator door?* Soft, muffled sounds drifted from the kitchen. Luke froze.

Someone was in his house.

Silent as a stalking panther, Luke eased off his couch and glided like a shadow into the adjacent room. He hadn't turned his alarm system on yet, but he had too many friends who knew too much about electronics, security, and international espionage. They had insisted on installing a video surveillance system in his house. The cameras were on twenty-four seven.

Quickly, he scanned the split screen on the large monitor. For a moment he couldn't move. His heart skipped a beat. She was in his house. Solid. Real. Classically beautiful, and not at all what he would've expected in a dream. Dressed in white from head to toe, she looked more like an angel than a thief. Capri pants. Short-sleeved shirt. Tennis shoes and bobby socks. She looked like a teenager on her way to a picnic. And she wasn't armed.

For a split second he wondered if he was dreaming. Had he fallen asleep on his couch?

Luke pinched himself. Hard. It hurt like hell. No. This was no dream, but a real, flesh and blood woman. The same woman he'd seen flickering in his peripheral vision so many times today, he'd thought he was going crazy. So, what the hell was she doing crawling around in his kitchen, stealing food? She didn't look homeless or malnourished. His gaze rested on the generous curves beneath her blouse. Quite the opposite. "Interesting."

The thought crossed his mind that he should be concerned. But he worked in a lethal environment on a daily basis. Life took on a whole new perspective. He never had the privilege of panic. This small, unarmed woman wasn't high on his worry list. He'd take his chances on her not being a true member of the heavenly host. If she struck him down with a lightning bolt, well he'd take it up with God when he saw him. But nothing was going to stop him from finding out what she was doing in his house.

He gave her no warning, just strolled into the kitchen, pulled open the refrigerator door, and turned around to where he knew she was sitting. "Anything in particular I can get for you?"

She gasped, her mouth forming a perfect ellipse, then disappeared into thin air. The smile he'd had in place to accompany the sarcasm fell like a two-ton rock and landed in his stomach. He shook his head to clear it, blinked several times. She was still gone. Vanished.

An angel, huh? Yeah, right. Years of Sunday school teachings were running rampant in his head. Maybe he was hallucinating. How many cups of coffee had he had today, anyway? Ten?

Fervently, he hoped she wasn't an angel. She was most definitely the woman he'd seen in his dreams. If she was an angel, he'd surely burn in hell for the things he'd fantasized about her.

No. She must be real. The camera couldn't lie. Neither could the heat in his chest.

The sound of glass shattering on the tile floor in his study broke the silence. The tight band around his chest eased. She was still here. Breaking things. He smiled. An angel wouldn't break furniture. "There went Grandmother's lamp."

He followed the sound to the dark doorway of his study and squinted into the inky blackness of the room. "Don't walk around. That lamp was glass." No response. Then crunching. Obviously, she wasn't a great listener. Slowly, enunciating every syllable, he took his voice up a couple of decibels. "I'm going to turn on the light. I'm not going to hurt you."

"No!"

The word froze him in place. He waited in the darkness while the silence stretched on. "Why are you in my house?" Silence. "And why were you following me around all day?"

Her quick gasp was his only indication that she'd heard him.

"I'm turning on the light now."

"Please don't." The words were more a resigned sigh than a request.

"Why not?"

"Because I'm not ready to talk to you yet."

Too bad. He'd been ready to talk to her for sixteen years. With a decisive flick of his wrist, he flipped the light switch up. He blinked a couple times as his eyes adjusted to the shocking glow of the naked bulb in his antique glass table lamp. The broken lamp was lying on the hardwood floor, its faceted body in shatters. At least it still worked.

The light coming up from the floor cast shadows in reverse on his angel's face. But was she an angel, or a beautifully seductive demon? And what was she doing here?

"Who are you and why are you in my house?"

Her clear blue eyes held censure, and fear. The fear held him in check and kept him silent. She eased around the edge of the desk and stood in front of the lamp. Once again, the shadows swallowed her face. He resisted the need to reach out and touch her skin, to make sure she was real and not some twisted game his imagination was playing to torture him.

Innocent but sassy. Sexy. Afraid. But of what?

"M-6." Her voice was a mere whisper of sound but it thundered through his mind, whirling and destroying his thoughts like a mental tornado.

"How do you know about M-6?" No one knew. The project was classified. The first shiver of real dread raced up his spine. How could she know? He grabbed her shoulders and pulled her small frame directly in front of him. "Who are you?"

She squirmed for a moment in protest and he loosened his grip, but didn't let go. She wasn't going anywhere until he had some answers. He couldn't risk her disappearing act again. If she escaped now, he'd truly believe he'd gone crazy. Lusting after a figment of your imagination for years was bad enough. Believing he'd held her in his arms and then lost her would make him certifiable. And he knew, beyond a shadow of a doubt, she was not a woman he could ever touch and then forget.

No, he intended to hang onto her for as long as he could. With a slow, measured breath he took the scent of her into his lungs. A mixture of roses and fresh rain. She smelled good. Too good. Exactly like his dreams. But this was no dream.

"The bug gets out, Luke. You have to help me kill it." She was staring him straight in the eye. In their depths he saw truth. And pity. The pity scared the hell out of him.

Ω

Chapter Three

The implications of her statement struck instantly, like a sledgehammer poised over his skull slamming home. This was a possibility everyone in the Hot Zone hypothesized, planned for, and prayed would never happen.

"I'm responsible?" Her slight assent shook him to the core. He crushed her so tightly to his chest he could barely breathe and hoped he was having a nightmare.

She didn't struggle, just waited, in silence. For over half his lifetime he'd waited, imagined her warm body pressed against his countless times. Now he was so ice cold inside he didn't think even she could warm him. He'd believed in her for years. His faith left plenty of room for him to have his own personal angel. But for what? To love him? To end his solitary existence?

No. To tell him he was going to kill people with his research. "How many? How far will it go?"

Small, delicate hands shoved at his chest as she pushed away to look up at him. "Everyone."

Beneath her, her legs buckled. But her weakness didn't register. Holding her up, he demanded more answers. "Everyone? How many?"

Her eyelashes dropped down to cover the truth in her eyes, the weakness. "Billions, Luke. Everybody. The whole world."

"No." He shook her gently. "I don't believe you." Every brain cell he had was firing, thinking, plotting, theorizing about how what she said could come to be. His mind wouldn't accept that any of this was happening. Gut instinct disagreed. The mass of twisting intestines roiling in his abdomen knew she was real. Knew she was telling him the truth. Knew, and didn't have a damn clue what to do about it.

"How do you know? How did you get in here?"

Slurred words were her only answer and he really looked at her for the first time. Her pale skin was translucent. The delicate snaking of vessels on her eyelids was acutely visible. Her eyes were brilliant blue, and so bloodshot he wondered how she could see at all. Her breathing was fast and shallow, and if he hadn't been holding onto her arms so tightly she would have fallen. "What's wrong with you?"

A wan smile served as her apology. "I need to eat."

Without another word, Luke carried her to the kitchen and settled her in a chair at his oak dining table. Praying she wouldn't topple over, he broke out his gourmet cooking skills and warmed up a can of tomato soup. Tears welled in her eyes when he set it and some crackers in front of her. He looked away, stared up at the marbled green and brown paint covering the walls and willed her tears not to fall. Hysterical women were not his forte. Hell, he should be the one in hysterics. If she was telling him the truth, he was taking the news pretty well. It wasn't every day a stranger told you that you were responsible for the end of the world.

He stalked to his coffee pot. "Damn it." Empty. Of course it was empty. It was after ten o'clock. He should be asleep, not wondering if this woman was real or a figment of his imagination. Warring parts of him were hoping for both.

He tried to be patient. For years he'd loved this woman, had obsessed about her so much in college his roommates had thought he'd lost his mind. More than one girlfriend had dumped him because he couldn't stop thinking about her. Countless drawings of her face were upstairs. But it wasn't supposed to be like this. He was supposed to meet her on the beach, or at a party, or… Hell. Anywhere.

"May I have something else?" Her voice sent warmth flowing back into his bloodstream.

"Sure." A little of her color was back. Good. Two microwave dinners, several sodas, a bag of chips, and two plums later she was finally done. When her knowing gaze settled on him once again, he almost wished she wasn't.

"Are you ready to hear the whole story?"

What choice did he have? All those years ago the man in a white robe had told him this woman would be his. That he would have to save her. Luke was convinced one of God's personal messengers had given him an assignment. He was equally sure he'd pay in hell if he failed. So would she.

"Go ahead." He sank down into the chair next to hers and hid his shaking hands under the table.

"My name is Alexa Antwyr. I was sent…here." Her eyes darted away from his face, then back again. "I was sent here to stop M-6 from escaping."

"Escaping what?"

"Your lab."

"This hasn't happened yet?"

She shook her head and he knew his eyes were widening in shock. "You expect me to believe you're from the future? Or some kind of prophet?"

"Yes."

He was about to say more, but she interrupted.

"In two days' time, you, several people you work with, and a man named Matthew Kline are going to be exposed to M-6. Within four weeks of that exposure you are all dead."

Two days. The date of the annual fundraising dinner. A couple hundred people would be there from all over the country. "How?"

"I don't know."

Luke's head was going to explode with the possibilities. "Just a handful of us would be easy to track and quarantine. How does it get to the rest of the world?"

"The party, they think. It spread like the flu and started mutating on its own. Hopped on airplanes and flew all over the country and the rest of the world before any of you showed any symptoms. They speculated that you crossed it with some kind of flu virus because it's airborne and hard to kill. Based on the three week incubation period, they decided May 9, was the day you were all first exposed."

"It's airborne?" That was a staggering realization. How many people could be exposed in twenty-one days? Twenty-one days when the carrier didn't know he was sick, or show signs of infection…and a cough could kill. "That's impossible."

"We don't know how he did it, but Trent crossed your strain of M-6 with some unknown type of influenza. That's their theory anyway."

"You're from the future and all you have is a damn theory?" His head was threatening to pound off of his neck and this was all just speculation? If she didn't look like a strong gust of wind would blow her over, he'd strangle her.

"No. I…" Her blue eyes held such sadness, such truth, he could barely bring himself to look at her. "There was no one left to record…"

"Stop." Luke ran his hand through his hair and studied her face, looking for something, anything that would convince him she didn't believe what she was telling him. He searched in vain. Nerves drove his fingertips to pound the tabletop. So, whoever sent Alexa to him thought Trent had mixed influenza with the Ebola mutation he'd been working with. Before today, he'd have laughed this woman out of his house. However, today Trent had laid out a plan eerily similar to what she was suggesting. Could Trent have gone in without his knowledge and started his pet project a little early? The hair rising on the back of his neck answered the question for him. "Okay. Start at the beginning and tell me everything."

Long, warm fingers wrapped around his on the tabletop, stopped their awkward beat. As much as he wanted to be strong, he couldn't pull away from the soft feminine touch. Her soft, confident voice whipped around, clearing the cobwebs of doubt, screaming inside his soul like a strong hot wind streaking through a canyon. "My name is Alexa Antwyr. I was sent back in time to stop the Red Death from wiping out this Earth."

"Red Death?"

She squeezed his hand. "That's what they called it after it got out."

The images her words brought to mind were horrifying. He'd seen Ebola outbreaks, worked for the CDC when they had a couple of outbreaks in Africa a few years ago. First time he'd been on the front lines and it wasn't pretty. The whole planet? "Did you say 'this Earth'?"

Nodding, she pulled her hand from his and stood. "Can we go outside? I'm not used to being stuck inside all day."

Escape. That was fine with him. Maybe it would be easier to hear about how he'd destroyed the entire world outside, in the dark, where he couldn't see her face. Luke led the way to his back porch swing, but didn't turn on the light. Instead of joining him, Alexa paced along the edge of his porch, her head thrown back to inhale the various aromas floating in the humid night sky. Roses. His neighbor's lilac bush. Fresh-cut grass and rhododendron blossoms. Her small delicate hands glided over the cedar porch railing and he wished like hell she was touching him that way. He wanted to run as far away from her as possible almost as much as he wanted her writhing naked beneath him. Not a good combination.

Enough adrenaline pumped through his system he figured he could go run a marathon and not even get warmed up. Or make love to her all night. He shifted uncomfortably. "All right, angel. Tell me the rest."

Alexa didn't answer him right away. She stared at him as if trying to come to some monumental decision.

"What does that look mean?" Her hands ran up and down her arms, despite the warm damp air that held them in its unrelenting heat. Fireflies danced behind her in the yard like small fairies come to worship their queen. Their silent queen. Luke prided himself on his self-control and patience. She was pushing the limits of both. "What aren't you telling me?"

"I can't decide whether or not to really trust you. Are you really going to help me destroy your life's work? Are you going to be able to accept the truth?" Her words rang in challenge and he realized she didn't truly believe he was going to help her. She didn't trust him. She couldn't know about all the nights he'd already spent with her in his mind. He knew a gift from heaven when he saw one. And he'd been waiting for her for one hell of a long time. The price tag attached to her appearance was getting steep, but not insurmountable. Yet. Already, he knew he was going to throw away his career to help her in her quest to save the world. And she was wondering if she could trust him? *Women.*

"I think it's pretty obvious we've both already made those decisions," Luke said. She'd broken into his home, eaten in his kitchen, plagued him in dreams for sixteen years, and she was wondering if he was going to believe in her? He'd been marked for her, for God's sake. He was going to do a whole hell of a lot more than that. For starters, he would see her naked in his bed, her body spread out before him like a pagan offering to the gods. He was going to worship at that altar all night. But first, there was the matter of saving a few lives.

He closed the distance between them slowly, like a big cat stalking his prey. His hands wrapped around her upper arms and he pulled her as close as he could without adding fuel to the fire by allowing their bodies to touch. There was only so much a man could take. "Alexa, I've known you for sixteen years. I'll do whatever it takes."

A quiver ran through her body and into his where he held her. He wondered for a moment if it was fear of him that caused it. Then he saw her pupils dilate with desire. Her tongue darted out to lick her lower lip. He'd wanted her in his dreams for so long that this felt like the thousandth time he'd touched her, not the first. Memories built into a tidal wave that carried him over the edge of control. He could no more resist those lips than force himself to stop dreaming of her. Luckily, the reality of her in his arms was so much better than his dreams.

He closed the distance between them. Slow. Deliberate. Her lips were millimeters from his own, still he waited. Savored the contact. Enjoyed the soft push of her full breasts against his chest. The moist heat of their mouths mingled in the air between them.

"Luke?" She whispered his name against his lips.

"Yes." The soft skin of her arms enticed his palms. He brushed the sensitive curves of her breasts through the thin white shirt as he slid his hands down her arms to settle on her hips. Heaven. She was pure heaven.

"I'm supposed to kill you."

He smiled and pulled her hips against his erection. *That* might kill him. "Can it wait?"

The smile was her undoing. It pulsed through the hot air that hovered between their mouths, wrapped around her heart and squeezed. Killing Luke Lawson was definitely out.

Rock hard chest muscles were hot beneath her wandering hands. Before wrapping her arms around his neck, she massaged every ounce of flesh. She buried her hands in the silky waves of his hair, exposing her body, inviting his touch to wander up from her hips to her breasts. Still he didn't close the distance between their mouths. She ached. Waited. Realized he was building the tension between them purposely. Her blood pounded in a wicked beat everywhere, throbbing. Especially between her legs, where she wanted him most.

"Kiss me." She didn't recognize the breathless need in her own voice.

"Thought you'd never ask."

Relief coursed through her until his hot mouth took possession of hers. Then she was on fire. Her world narrowed to him. His lips. The unforgiving muscles of his chest pressed against her hard nipples. He splayed his hands and slid them up and down her hips, so agonizingly close to where she wanted him to be, to touch. He invaded her mouth with his tongue, glided in and out, surrounded her with heat. The taste of him drove every sane thought from her head. A driving need to taste him forced her tongue to dart into his mouth to explore. To stake a claim.

A trail of fire burned over her where his hands slid around to cup her buttocks. He lifted her slightly, rubbing her against his arousal. She thought she would die with sweet pain. Her body wanted, needed him inside of her, filling her. Inner muscles pulsed to life, throbbed in desperate invitation. She arched back against the porch railing, forcing her body more firmly against his.

Hot lips traced her pulse down her neck. He nibbled at her shoulder and torturous pulses of shock rippled through her, to her very core. She was going into meltdown. "Luke."

His only answer was to lift her higher, until her nipple hung suspended in front of the searing heat of his mouth. Unable to resist, she pulled him to her. A soft moan escaped her lips when he softly bit the peak through her thin cotton shirt. Her legs wrapped around his waist, his body her only anchor in a hurricane of sensations more intense than anything she'd ever experienced.

One of his hands moved to her waist, then up beneath her shirt. Sweet torture glided over her flesh as his hands teased, grazed her skin with the lightest touch, and finally pushed the offending fabric to bunch at her shoulders. Exposed, her nipple was peaked and hard, begging for more. His tongue found her first, flicked. Then he closed his mouth around the mound, sucked until she moaned his name.

Her entire body tuned to the accelerated beat of her heart. Throbbing with need. Burning through her skin where the mark of her calling was now blazing with a life of its own. With his tongue, he found the heated birthmark on her breast and traced the hot design, searing the symbol into her consciousness. Branding her as his forever.

Her birthmark. Her heritage. Her destiny.

"Stop." It was going to kill her, and probably him too, but they couldn't do this. Not yet. Every lecture she'd ever had from her mother had touched on this subject. Her mother must have known what it would be like for her, once she met Luke. Memories of heated gazes that constantly passed between her mother and father jumped to the fore. Judging by her parent's relationship, this thing between them wasn't ever going to cool down. But they had work to do first. She wasn't going to fail because this man drove every drop of blood from her head to other parts of her body.

"Luke, I'm sorry." Gathering every ounce of self-control she'd ever had, she unwrapped her legs from his waist and slid back down the hard length of him to stand on the porch. Still exposed, her nipple slid along his chest on the way down, and she gritted her teeth at the bittersweet agony. "We have to stop."

He didn't answer, just rested his head against hers with his eyes closed and stilled his roving hands. They rested on her hips, torturing her with their heat through her thin cotton Capris.

"I'm sorry." She felt like the worst kind of tease. But she was suffering too.

Her hands had a mind of their own and still explored the planes of his chest. His body was too close, too hard, too tempting. She pushed away from him and hurried over to the cushioned porch swing. Legs curled beneath her, she sat on her hands so she couldn't reach for him, and watched Luke get himself under control. Gradually both of their breathing rhythms returned to normal. Unconsciously, her hand moved to her chest and massaged the still pulsing symbol there. The symbol her daughter, *their* daughter, would carry.

When his eyes finally opened, his attention was immediately drawn to the hand over her heart. "What does the mark mean?"

Alexa lifted one shoulder in a quick shrug. "It's a birthmark. The Shen, my mother called it." For probably the thousandth time in her life, she traced the half-inch ring with her fingertip. Such a simple mark. Her mother said it was a rope looped around. No beginning. No end. It looked like a circle sitting atop a straight line. How she'd hated that mark growing up. Kept it hidden. Resented what it meant. Only when the Archiver's call had come had she begun to understand the honor. And the cost. "It means eternity and protection in a language so old and powerful only the Archivers are trusted with the knowledge." Their gazes locked and held in the shadows. “It’s the mark of the Taken.”

“The Taken?”

“Yes. I've been told that Timewalkers and Archivers carry the mark. As do their descendants.” He seemed to be taking this pretty well, considering. But what had he said earlier? She almost regretted the fact that her brain had begun to function again. “Did you say you’ve known me for sixteen years?”

“Yes.”

That was all she got out of him. Great. Come to think of it, he hadn’t said more than about two words the entire time. He was accepting all this much too easily. “How?”

“My dreams.”

Had he truly dreamt of her? She struggled to speak over the lump in her throat. “What kind of dreams?”

“When the time comes, I’ll be happy to show you. Until then, don’t ask if you aren’t ready for the answer.” Luke’s smile melted her insides and she was thankful the semi-darkness covered the flush rising on her face.

“So, you knew I was coming?”

His gaze locked her to him, the intensity she saw in his eyes left her unable to move, or breathe. Like a predator, he came to kneel before her and started to unbutton his shirt. Her pulse skyrocketed. The hard back of the swing stopped her retreat. Trapped. “What are you doing?”

Now open to his waist, Luke pulled his shirt aside. Suddenly, Alexa wished the porch light was on. He grabbed her hand and pulled it, slowly, toward his heart. “I didn’t know you would find me.”

He pressed her palm to his heated skin, to the flesh she desperately needed to taste. Alexa closed her eyes to keep herself from lunging at him. An unnatural heat radiated beneath her palm, pulsing in time to her own throbbing birthmark. She gasped in shock and lifted her hand to inspect his chest in the dim light shining from the window behind her. There, branded into his flesh, was a mark that exactly matched her own. "How -- ?" Once again, she met his gaze and another rush of heat threatened her self-control. "Your dreams?"

He nodded. "Sometimes, I thought I was crazy. But after the first dream, I woke up with this." Hand locked over hers, he cradled her palm against the mark on his chest. "So, I didn't know you were coming, but I was promised. And I hoped."

"I can be a difficult woman to deal with." She pulled her hand away from the gentle seduction of his caressing fingers, the nearly irresistible call of the mark on his skin.

"I'll take my chances." His snort made her want to jump up off the swing and show him just how difficult she could be. She held herself in check. Barely. What was wrong with her? Her moods were never this mercurial. With eight younger brothers, she was used to much worse.

Hormones. She hated hormones. And the meddling of a jerk in white. How dare he choose a mate for her, brand him, and then tell her she may have to kill him? There could be no doubt now. He was hers.

A Cheshire cat grin fell into place on her face. "Listen. I won't deny that I would love to go roll around naked with you and explore this…" She searched for a word to describe the miniature explosions that happened inside her body every time she even looked at him. "…attraction between us."

"Attraction?" Six feet of pure temptation slid onto the seat next to her. She pulled back from his warmth as if burned. He had the nerve to notice. And grin.

"Yes, attraction."

His long index finger reached out and rubbed the sensitive skin above her knee through her pants. "I like the rolling around naked idea."

God, so did she. She bit into her lower lip. Hard. She wished he'd button that damn shirt. His hand lifted from her knee to caress her cheek before he spoke.

"Come inside. There's something I want to show you."

Ω
Chapter Four

Strong hands enveloped hers and led her through the dark hallway. Blindly, she followed, taking on faith that the Archiver knew what he was doing when he chose Luke to be her mate. Already, his body lit hers on fire. He'd listened, promised to help her, and hadn't accused her of being crazy. Three big marks in his favor.

"Close your eyes." Luke backed into a darkened room, pulling her inside after him. She grinned in anticipation and allowed her eyelids to drift down. When she was somewhere in the middle of the room, he left her. "Don't move, and don't open your eyes."

"All right."

Like a whisper, he moved past her back toward the door leaving her alone in the shadows. Light burst through her closed eyelids, tinged pink from passing through her flesh. Her toe tapped impatiently as she waited for the command to see. Luke's warm body pressed into her back and she inhaled sharply. Eyes open, he was enticing. Eyes closed, pure sensation ruled and Luke Lawson was devastating to the senses. Her body hummed with awareness. The emptiness she'd felt before flared back to life with a vengeance.

Hot breath tickled her ear, her neck, sending shivers racing down her spine.

"Okay. Open your eyes."

"Oh, my God." Nothing could've prepared her for this. Four large canvasses covered the wall in front of her. Lovingly drawn, in exquisite detail, was her face. Four different angles. Four different expressions. But her, right down to the tiny mole on her cheek and the small scar over her left eye. The scar was a gift her brother, Bryne, gave her when she was eight years old. Her legs were so weak, only the intoxicating arms wrapped around her waist held her upright. "How did you…?"

"There's more." Gently, he turned her to the opposite wall. There, much smaller but no less detailed, was a perfect rendering of every member of her family. Everyone she loved was on that wall, dispersed between framed black and white photographs of nature. Scattered. Faces she thought to never see again.

White-hot pokers stabbed behind her eyelids. Her head felt like it was being squeezed by a giant fist. Deep inside her chest, her heart actually hurt. Oh, how she loved them all. Missed them. Now she'd never forget their faces, never forget the people who were everything to her. This gift Luke gave her was priceless, and filled with love. Tears streaked her face, but she didn't fight them, didn't close her eyes to trap them inside. Greedily, her gaze roamed the room. Luke's arms tightened around her waist.

"Do you like them?"

She tried to answer, but a soft sob was all that managed to break through the tightness of her throat. Luke turned her to face him. With a lover's tender touch, he wiped away her tears with his thumbs. Worry creased his brow.

"I'm sorry, Alexa. Maybe I should've waited to show this to you."

"No." Turning her head, she kissed the palm of first one hand, then his other. "Thank you."

"You're welcome. But it wasn't supposed to make you cry."

He looked genuinely upset at her reaction. Heaven help her. She was pretty damn sure she'd just fallen head over heels in love with the man. And she wanted to make love to him. Right now. To hell with waiting. He was hers. He'd been *branded!* Not to mention that they might both be dead in a few weeks anyway. She wanted every precious moment she could get.

Fingers curled around the hem of her shirt, she lifted it off over her head. His hungry gaze devoured her naked flesh. Stepping close, she slid her hands up his chest and shoved the already gaping white dress shirt off his shoulders. He shrugged out of it and pulled her roughly against him. With a soft moan, she pulled his head down to hers, tasted his lips, his tongue, before sliding down to caress the mark on his chest with her tongue.

The Shen pulsed with heat beneath her tongue. Hers answered, sent an electric shock straight to her core.

Luke's hands slid over the bare skin of her back. His thumbs linked in the waistband of her pants. Stopped. "Now will you admit that you're mine?"

"Yes." *He* was *hers,* but she could remind him of that fact later. Right now, his scent filled her nostrils. The emptiness of her body ached to be filled by his.

His lips nibbled a trail of fire down her neck, over her collarbone. Cupping her breasts in his palms, he teased her nipples into hard peaks. "Tell me what you want."

"You."

"Good." That fast her gentle lover was gone. Shoving her pants down her legs, he dragged her lace thong with them. When she tried to step out of them he simply lifted her off her feet and crushed her to him. He took command with his mouth, tasted, invaded, demanded a response while one hand cupped her bottom, held her throbbing core against his cock. Frantic, she tugged at his pants. She needed him inside of her, filling the emptiness.

"Not so fast." Luke laughed at her, lifted her to raze her nipples with his five o'clock shadow as he carried to another room, to his bed. "I've waited a long time for this."

She didn't notice much. Sparse furniture of dark wood. Huge windows flooded with moonlight. Dark sheets that felt like silk beneath her heated skin when he laid her across the bed. For a moment he left her, then returned, naked. Hard. Ready. Alexa held out her arms and he covered her with his body, crushing her into the pillow-top mattress.

A sigh of pure relief escaped. Then he took possession once again. Dominant, his mouth captured hers, ruled. Sliding lower, he kissed her stomach before lifting his body off to her side. Sucking one nipple into his mouth, he gently nibbled with his teeth. She arched up off the bed, needing more. He sent one hand to wander over the smooth plane of her stomach, then lower to cup her moist heat, to grind his palm against her. His mouth wandered over her rib cage, down the soft plane of her stomach. Lower. One hand pulled her folds apart, offering her throbbing nub up for attention. Hot, hard, his tongue stroked the sensitive flesh while he slowly pushed two fingers from his other hand inside.

Alexa's only thought was that she was going to die of pleasure. Without conscious thought, she shoved her hips against him, pushed forcefully against the dual onslaught of his hands and mouth. She moaned. She writhed. She whimpered with need.

Relentless, savage, he claimed complete ownership of her body. Flicking faster, the heat of his mouth incinerated her flesh. Moving in and out, his fingers stroked her to a frenzy. When she was close to shattering, his mouth closed over her, sucked, pulled rhythmically. Deep inside, he attacked the tip of her womb with his fingers, rubbed against her deepest core until she shattered in his arms.

Without giving her a chance to breath again, he inched his way up her body, rubbed his heated skin over hers, settled his hips in the cradle of hers. She lifted her hips in welcome, giving him a better angle. Moving feverishly, he coated himself with her juices before ramming home in one strong thrust.

Searing heat leapt between their Shen, binding them together. Alexa felt the difference in her body, knew she'd be able to find Luke anywhere on this earth. Bonded until death. Luke moved harder, faster, burying himself so deeply inside of her she knew she'd never get him out. The power of the Shen surged through them, heightened their senses and sizzled their blood, until her body exploded with pleasure. The muscles of her core clenched and pulsed around him, pulled him over the edge with her.

* * *

"I'll go in alone. I don't want you in there." Luke knew he looked like a fool whispering to himself as he walked down the hallway. He didn't care. Alexa could hear him. Her hand was scorching the skin on his shoulder where she hung onto him, making him remember things he'd rather not be thinking about right now. Like her…naked.

She pinched him.

He paused at the door to the men's locker room, then punched in the security code. How had she talked him into this? He should've left her at home, like he'd wanted to. There wasn't a chance in hell he was going to risk her life, or anyone else's, by allowing her into the Hot Zone. But he hadn't thought of the locker room. The thought of her looking at the other naked men made him crazy. Undressing himself, knowing she was watching. Wishing she'd touch him. Wondering if she would.

This was a terrible idea. Time to turn around and drive her home.

As if she could read his thoughts, she shoved him through the door and three friendly faces looked up in greeting. They were all partially undressed, their clothes thrown haphazardly into the steel lockers. He hurried to the far side of the room and the oversized locker with his name on it. Gritting his teeth, he fumbled with the combination lock. Cold awareness nearly made him shudder when her hand abandoned his shoulder. Now he had no idea where she was, what she was doing. Who she was looking at.

The friendly banter of his buddies didn't help his mood. He tried to sound normal, to speak when spoken to, but he wasn't sure how successful he was. They were all going in to feed the mutants this morning. Make sure all the cultures were growing. Count bacterial colonies. Count cells. Count petri dishes. Count death.

With great care, he peeled the clothing from his body slowly, thankful for all the hours he'd spent in the gym. Hoping she was watching, he took his time and made damn sure the others were gone by the time his pants came off. They'd all wonder why the hell he had an erection if they saw him. He hoped Alexa saw him. Saw him, and wanted him slamming home.

Get a grip, Lawson. He had a job to do. The sooner he destroyed all the mutant cultures, the sooner he could pursue his other, much more enjoyable, interests.

His research career with the Army was going to be over after today. Today he was going to deliberately break an order. He had pending orders to destroy M-6, but he was going to jump the gun a little. In light of everything Alexa told him last night, his career was irrelevant. Money wasn't an issue. More than enough was stashed in investment accounts. He'd get a job teaching at a university. Something low key. Low stress. Somewhere a single mistake couldn't get him, and the rest of the world, killed.

He'd found heaven with Alexa last night, holding her in his arms while she slept. Lying there, awake all night, his fingertips memorized the soft curves of her face while his analytical mind pieced together their future. Afraid to go to sleep. Afraid if he did, when he woke up, she'd be gone.

That's why he'd been so easy to persuade this morning. She insisted this was her mission and she needed to see it through. Only one thing had swayed him into allowing her to tag along. Plain and simple, he didn't want her out of his sight.

Hell of a lot of good that logic was doing him now. He couldn't see her anyway.

The other men moved into the next room to suit up. Alone at last. "Alexa, I want you to wait in here. Don't move. It shouldn't take me more than a half hour to get them all in the oven."

Silence.

"Alexa?"

Cold fear squeezed Luke's diaphragm, making it difficult to breath the canned air. She wouldn't. If she went in there… She didn't have any training in the suits. She was going to get them all killed. "Shit." Pulling his pants off in a frenzy, he threw them in the general direction of his locker. He wanted to strangle her. But even more powerful than his anger was his fear that he'd lose her. "God, woman. You're going to get yourself killed."

"Relax. I'm not an idiot."

All the air left his lungs in a giant whoosh. Alexa was taking him on one hell of a roller coaster ride. The touch of her hand on his bare shoulder jolted him back into high gear like an electric current. "Don't even think about going in there."

"I admit, I was going to try. But after your lecture last night, I'd have to be suicidal to go in there with no training." Soft, delicate, her hand glided down his back to linger on his left buttock.

"Damn right." There was only so much torture a man could take. Whirling around, he grabbed at the spot where he knew she must be standing. Closing his arms around her soft frame, he pulled her to rest against his naked flesh.

"This was a bad idea." Shimmering into view, she locked her blue eyes onto his. "I'm sorry. I'll be a good girl now and wait out in the hallway."

"Too late." Lowering his lips to hers, he breathed a question into her mouth. "Do you like what you see?"

After a quick kiss she shoved him away from her. "Go."

He reached for her, but she vanished. In vain he tried to grab her, but she was bent on hiding from him now. Her voice echoed off the cold tile floor. "Go. Kill them all, Luke. Kill every single one of them."

Why did thirty minutes have to feel like an eternity in this cold locker room where her own heartbeat echoed too loudly in her ears? She hoped she wasn't making a mistake, trusting Luke to finish it. But she couldn't go in there. She didn't know how to put on the suit or run the equipment. She didn't know where the cultures were kept or how to destroy them. Not a chance in hell she was going in there. Talk about a fish out of water! A guppy flopping around in a room so dangerous just breathing the air would kill her. "C'mon Luke." Raw nerves drove her sandaled feet across the cold tile floor. Back and forth. Waiting.

She didn't dare let down her guard and allow her cloak of invisibility to fall. Anyone could walk through that door at any time. The men's locker room wasn't somewhere she wanted to be found.

Might be a little tough explaining to someone what she was doing in here. But holding the energy pattern was beginning to take its toll. Her eye was twitching again. It wouldn't be long before she was blinking in and out of sight. Before that happened, she had to be out of the building.

A loud rush of sound alerted her that the decontamination showers were on. *Thank God.* Six minutes of chemical disinfectants pounding him inside the suit. Then he'd be back in the locker room, naked. Heat rose to her cheeks. Her pulse leapt. The memory of her breasts sliding against his hard body drove every sane thought from her head and made her birthmark heat up. "Stop it. Stop it. Stop it." There was no time for this. They had a job to do. Her feet quickened the pace and she bit her knuckles.

The breath she'd been holding escaped in a rush when the door finally opened. Wearing nothing but a towel slung low over those sexy hips, he stepped into the room. "Alexa?"

"I'm here." Her voice sounded strangled, even to her, and she was glad he couldn't see her staring at the sculpted muscles she was dying to touch.

He didn't appear to notice anything wrong with her voice and didn't bother trying to look for her. "We have a problem, angel." First he ran his hand through his damp hair, then rubbed a kink in his neck. "I destroyed everything in there, but two of the cultures are missing."

Like a shock of cold water dumped on her steaming libido, his words sank in. She shook her head. No. This couldn't happen. "Trent."

"Yes." Luke strolled over to his locker and pulled his shirt on. "The other guys told me he was really worked up when he came in earlier this morning."

"Why?"

After pulling a pair of boxers on underneath the fluffy white towel he threw the towel onto the floor. "He got canned."

Shaking her head, she tried in vain not to stare at Luke's bare legs. What did that mean? "I don't understand that term. What's canned?"

"They fired him. Took him off the project. Gave him his walking papers. Told him to get his shit and get out. Canned."

Alexa was surprised the seams in his pants didn't rip open, Luke was shoving his legs into them with such force. "His employment was terminated? Why?"

"Because I had to be an ass and make a few phone calls."

Was Luke clenching his teeth? She drifted closer, close enough to touch him, but didn't. "I don't understand."

"I don't either." Fully dressed and ready to go, he slammed his locker closed. "Damn it! They weren't supposed to do this until after tomorrow night. I guess the Colonel hated him too much to wait."

Tomorrow night was the big party. The time and place, it was believed, where the Red Death launched its attack on the world. "So, Trent got mad and managed to walk out of here with M-6? Why? What's he going to do with it?"

"Sell it, probably. He's the only one who could've taken the cultures. I'm sorry"

Her knees buckled and she sank down onto the hard metal bench. "We have to find him." The bug was out. She'd failed. And now, they only had twenty-four hours left to find Trent and stop him from killing them all.

"Damn it. I hate this. Where the hell are you?"

Alexa gladly allowed her energy pattern to return to normal. The moment she did, he pulled her into his arms.

Her mind in turmoil, Alexa rested her head against Luke's chest and allowed the steady beating of his heart to calm her. Hell. It looked like she was going to have to kill a man after all. Trent had to be stopped. She couldn't let anyone, or anything, stand in her way. And that included her own traitorous heart.

Reluctantly, she disentangled herself from his embrace. "Who's he going to sell it to?"

"I have no idea." Luke looked like he wanted to reach for her again, but thought better of it. "But he'll be at the fundraiser tomorrow. That's where the initial outbreak takes place."

Alexa nodded. "How would you like to be my escort tomorrow evening?"

His smile turned her bones to jelly. "We're going to need a plan. It's not too late to stop this thing."

"What I'm going to need is a dress for the party." And a gun. *Definitely a gun.*

Ω

Chapter Five

"How long should we wait out here?" Alexa asked. They'd been parked a half block away from Trent's home for over an hour. It was after midnight and they hadn't seen any sign of him. Alexa shifted uncomfortably in the soft leather bucket seat next to Luke and looked through his binoculars toward Trent's two-story colonial style home. The house was new, but built to look old. Red brick spanned the front and was accented by two white columns. Climbing rosebushes and vines covered the front of the home up to the top of the first floor windows. Several lights were on, but every single curtain was closed.

"Hell, I don't know. Let me check my spy handbook."

The annoyed look she cast his way made him want to kiss her. Before he could, she focused her attention on the house again. "Got a copy of 'Breaking And Entering For Dummies'?"

"This isn't funny, you know."

"I know."

Of its own volition, his right hand caressed her neck and his thumb feathered over her left cheek. As hard as he tried, he couldn't stop touching her, couldn't stop thinking about her. She was the only thing standing between the entire world and Death. And she'd trusted him. It was humbling. And terrifying.

Lightning quick, she pressed a kiss into his palm, then opened her door. "I'll be back."

She was out of the vehicle before he could protest, her black slacks and shirt melting into the shadows. If not for her hair, he'd have lost track her. Then, with a little wave, she vanished. "Damn it." How was he supposed to keep her out of trouble if she kept disappearing? At least this time he knew where she was going.

When he reached Trent's back door, he was rewarded by the sound of Alexa's sexy voice cursing, and the door handle rattling. "Need a little help?"

"You were supposed to wait in the car."

A chuckle escaped, despite the situation. "Sit still like a good boy while you go in there and get yourself killed? Not in this lifetime, angel." He hated talking to air.

"But they can see you."

"Yeah, and we're all dead tomorrow anyway."

Apparently she didn't have a sassy comeback for that. Alexa reappeared in front of him and he sighed in relief. So far, she'd had no luck picking the lock. Then he heard a soft click and her soft sigh of relief. "Finally."

The heavy oak door swung open silently and they both tensed in anticipation of an alarm sounding. Instead, an unnatural silence crept out of the house to envelop them in its cold embrace. The alarm panel next to the door stared back at them with an eerie green glow.

Worried blue eyes flashed back at him over Alexa's shoulder. "Something's wrong."

He wanted to argue, but couldn't. The very air seemed to dread their entry. Sliding his arm around her waist he forced her behind him. "I don't suppose you'd go wait in the car?"

She tried to shove past him, but he tightened his grip. "Stay behind me…and disappear."

The house was wrecked. Expensive artwork torn off the walls and smashed over antique chairs in the front room. Tables overturned. Lamps shattered. Plush couch cushions embroidered with scenes of nineteenth century social life, ripped to shreds. Dishes in pieces on the paisley patterned carpeting. Even the drywall was punched through. Holes of various sizes dotted the walls in a haphazard fashion where someone had obviously used a sledgehammer with gusto. Spray paint adorned two walls in the dining room with curse words and juvenile insults. Luke shook his head. "Looks like kids."

Alexa's disembodied voice answered from the other side of the formal dining room. "That's what they wanted it to look like."

"Maybe." He had a bad feeling about this. "Alexa, go back outside. Don't touch anything. I'll look around."

Silence.

"Alexa?"

"I'm not leaving." Her answer drifted to him from another room. Was she upstairs? His gaze darted to the circular staircase that hugged the left side of the marble-floored foyer.

"Shit." He sprinted up the stairs two at a time.

In contrast, the second story was pristine. Gilded mirrors and paintings decorated the walls in precisely measured intervals. Artificial flowers sat undisturbed in imported vases that lined the hallway like sentinels resting on the hardwood floors. The quiet was more pronounced here, the well paid for perfection of their surroundings drove the silence home like an exclamation point at the end of a sentence. All the doors were closed. All but one. "Alexa?"

Where was she? His instincts screamed at him that someone was up here, waiting for her. Thank the Lord she was invisible to the naked eye. With her penchant for rushing headlong into trouble he hoped that ability would be enough to keep her from getting killed.

He crept closer to the open doorway and was almost glad she didn't answer. If he didn't know where she was, no one else would either.

The one open door loomed in front of him and he stood to the side for a moment, just listening. Silence. He slid into the room and looked around. Two ivory reading chairs and a burgundy loveseat huddled around a gas fireplace along one wall. Thick navy carpeting muffled his footsteps as he walked over to the sprawling antique desk across the room. The middle wall was covered in windows and floor to ceiling bookshelves decorated with leather-bound volumes of the classics. Books he was sure Trent had never read. But then, it was obvious that appearances meant everything to Trent. The entire house was a testament to his social ambitions.

The computer was humming where it sat in the shadows beneath the desk. He took two more steps before he saw the trails of dark liquid that splattered and slid down the front of the flat screen monitor. Artificial light flashed beneath the splatter pattern, casting a strange glow on the wall behind the desk.

Luke's legs stopped of their own accord. He knew what he was going to find, knew, and didn't want to permanently sear the image into his consciousness by looking.

Like a ghost come back to life, Alexa came into focus beside the desk. The shock in her eyes told him what she would say before she spoke to confirm it. "I think he's dead."

So much for ending this thing tonight. Trent's death would multiply their problems by a factor of ten.

Alexa jumped back with a yelp.

He rushed to her side, blood pounding in his ears.

"He moved."

If there was one thing he did *not* want to do, it was look down. Resigned, he dropped his gaze just as Trent's fingers curled around his pant leg like giant blood stained leeches. "Shit."

"Luke." Trent choked and sputtered where he laid flat on his back, then spit blood onto the floor. "He took it. I'm sorry."

Dropping to one knee beside Trent, he attempted to see beyond the blood. His boss had been shot multiple times. Chest. Stomach. Head. It was a miracle he was still alive. But he wouldn't be for long. "Alexa, find me a phone."

"No. Too late. Just listen." Trent grabbed Luke's forearm in a death grip. "Get the case back. He's crazy."

"Who?" Trent's fingernails cut into his skin but he barely noticed. The only thing that mattered was finding out who had the virus now.

"Kline."

Matthew Kline. He remembered the name from Alexa's tale.

Matthew was the man with whom he shared the privilege of being among the first to die. "Who is he?"

"He lied. Tomorrow. The Plaza. He said…" Trent rolled onto his side and blood slowly poured from his open lips like thick red syrup. The warm liquid slurred his words. "…we deserved it."

Luke knew enough to realize that Trent's stomach was filling with blood. Probably his lungs too. The paramedics couldn't make it in time. "Why?"

Trent's eyes closed, his last words were a sigh of surrender. "For playing God."

Numb, empty, Luke stared down at the dead man's face. If anyone had been playing God, he had. He'd created the monster and Trent had been killed for it.

Still staring at Trent, he was vaguely aware of Alexa as she unplugged Trent's computer, kicked the side panel off, and smashed everything inside with her black boot heel. After just a minute silence once again surrounded them. His little time traveler was efficient.

"Luke?" Alexa whispered from somewhere behind him.

Luke ignored her, gave his analytical mind a minute to catch up to the horror staring at him through Trent's lifeless eyes. What a mess! The M-6 was missing. Now Trent was murdered. This was rapidly getting out of hand. Who could he call? Would the Colonel believe any of this? Even if he left Alexa out of the story, the entire thing would sound paranoid. He now had a dead body and the missing cultures to back up his claims. Or get him locked away forever. The Colonel would believe him. But how quickly could the Colonel mobilize a team? And would they help or hurt his and Alexa's chances of stopping this thing? He couldn't just call the police. The Mutant Project was classified above top-secret. Word leaked out and there'd be mass hysteria. Streetwide panic. Shit would hit the fan so far up the food chain it would be a national scandal.

"Luke!" Her panic laced whisper caught his attention and Luke sprang to his feet.

"What?"

"Someone's still here." She jerked her head in the direction of the hallway.

"Give me your gun." He closed the distance and pushed her behind him. Shock widened her eyes and made him smile, despite the dire situation. "Relax. I'm not an idiot either."

Without hesitation, she grabbed the gun from her ankle holster, but refused to give it to him. "I'm an expert marksman. Are you?"

"I'm not bad." He was an excellent shot, but he didn't want to leave her unprotected. Her raised eyebrows told him she wasn't buying it. She handled the gun with such ease it seemed like a natural extension of her hand. Better to keep her safe. If he had to take someone out, he'd have to do it the old-fashioned way...with his bare hands.

"You think my mother would send me off into the big bad universe with no training at all? I could kick your ass right now or shoot you from a block away. My fingerprints aren't on any government database, either."

The woman had a point about the fingerprints. Then she darted past him into the hallway, and disappeared into thin air. "Damn it."

"Come on." Her voice was drifting toward the staircase just a few feet away. "He's downstairs. Let's see if we can get this guy and get the hell out of here."

Who could argue with that logic? When he reached the staircase a blinking red light caught his eye. Seconds later a steady beeping filled the house. "Alexa, he tripped the alarm." Motion detectors he'd paid no attention to suddenly blinked down on them with evil red eyes from every corner as if they knew their master was dead. "We gotta get out of here. Now!"

Neither spoke while they raced from the house. Alexa watched him wipe her fingerprints off of the back door handle, and then followed behind him like a shade, darting from shadow to shadow, sprinting back to his Cherokee.

Next to him, Alexa flinched when the engine's roar was a thunderclap on the silent street. Luke pulled away from the curb, turned the Jeep around, and headed home. When they were a safe distance from Trent's house, Alexa stirred on the seat beside him. "That went well."

"We're not dead, yet, angel." Not the most comforting words, but the truth. "We know where he's going with it, and I have friends who can help us."

Strain was lining her forehead and draining the color from her already pale face. Leaning her head back against the headrest she closed her eyes. "We've got less than twenty-four hours."

Ω
Chapter Six

Alexa knew Luke would disapprove. She wasn't in the mood to argue with him about it so she sat across from him inside the car with her mouth shut and counted the minutes. This was her mission. Her only reason for existence. If that meant she had six-inch knives strapped to both thighs and her 9mm handgun on her ankle, so be it. If she had to shoot a few people at the party to make sure no one walked out of there infected with M-6, then, so help her God, she was going to do it.

That included herself and Luke. She'd never been much for praying, but if she were forced to kill a man in cold blood to save the world, and then rot in prison on this planet for the rest of her life she was going to need all the help she could get when it was time to pull the trigger.

The car stopped and their driver opened the door for her. As much as she hated herself for it, she fled the confined space and Luke's knowing gaze like a panicked rabbit would flee a fox.

"You look beautiful." Luke stepped out of the rented limousine behind her onto the sidewalk in front of the Frost Bank Tower and lightly caressed her arm. He looked drop-dead gorgeous in his tuxedo. No pun intended. "The dress is perfect."

"Thank you." What was the use in playing coy? She knew she looked good. But last time she'd checked, being beautiful wouldn't help her stop a psycho.

What she needed was to stay calm, centered. Beneath this killer dress was her 9mm Lady Remington. Stuffed inside a matching clutch she had several rounds of ammunition. Hiding a large number of bullets had posed a problem so she'd left most of them behind. Standing there yesterday afternoon, listening to the pawnshop salesman sell his wares to the visible customers, she'd concluded that she couldn't kill that many people anyway. She might be forced to hold them all prisoner in quarantine and watch them die of Red Death, but she couldn't shoot innocent victims in cold blood. Even though a shot through the heart would be a more merciful ending.

No. She was just going to have to stop Matthew Kline before he had a chance to infect them all at the party. Putting a bullet into his fanatical skull would be less of a moral challenge.

Looking good when she put him out of his misery was just an added little bonus. She guessed she just had a little too much of her mother in her. And the testosterone of nine men in the house to contend with growing up. Dressing up was always fun.

She'd swept her hair up into a sexy chignon that exposed her long neck and made her hope Luke would find an excuse to kiss the sensitive skin there. The dress was the same pale blue as her eyes, like an arctic glacier, and shimmered when she moved. The layered material was so soft, it felt like rose petals beneath her fingertips. More importantly, it didn't make a sound when she moved. Delicate spaghetti straps bared her shoulders and drew attention to the translucent wrap of the same material that she draped around her shoulders and over her arms. The bodice hugged her body in waves until it reached the flare of her hips, then the dreamy material fell straight to the floor. She looked demure, innocent, and still had room under the skirt to hide her gun.

Only one thing ruined the whole effect, pantyhose. Horrible disgusting things. That was one thing she'd hoped hadn't been invented in this dimension. Why didn't they send someone back through time to prevent that thinly veiled attack against women?

Luke's gentle hand on the small of her back guided her to the entryway, and shot her temperature up by about a thousand degrees. Silently, he escorted her past the doorman and onto the elevator. Twenty-first floor. The Plaza Club. Private. Exclusive. Expensive. Alexa hadn't been able to grasp why they would spend so much money to try to raise money for their organization. It seemed like a stupid thing to do, but it wasn't her party. She was just crashing it.

The moment they stepped off the elevator Luke pulled her into a semi-private alcove. "Remember, the case is small. Like a kid's school lunchbox. Silver."

Alexa nodded, and tried to peek up over his shoulder at the people beginning to arrive at the entrance to the main dining hall. Luke's hands rested on her shoulders, then slowly caressed her skin, moving up and down her arms. His hands were sexy. Strong. Perfect. Every damn thing about him was perfect. Distracting. It was getting on her nerves. Who had time to be hot and bothered every single moment? She had a job to do.

"The Colonel and his men are already here. They've all seen the picture of Kline, too. They're trained killers, professionals, and they don't want this bug to get out either. They're here to help us."

She snorted at that and tried to ignore the way her birthmark flared to life when his strong hands wrapped around her wrists, holding her to him. The Colonel and two of his men had spent the entire afternoon at Luke's house, forcing her to either hide, or drain her energy by cloaking her presence. Despite her protests, Luke insisted they needed his help and called him. She'd disliked the pompous old ass at first sight. As far as she was concerned, he was responsible for this entire fiasco. This Mutant Project, as they called it, was his baby. The Colonel was the one who'd pitched it, funded it, and made enemies. Enemies who now appeared to be working with Trent. What did he think he was playing at? Viral DNA was not synonymous with 'tinker toy.'

"He's a pompous ass."

Luke laughed softly and planted a quick kiss on her lips. "Maybe. But I think his heart's in the right place."

"We'll see. I still say he didn't tell you everything."

Luke shrugged. "Nothing we can do about it now."

"I know." But she sure as hell was going to try.

Luke slid his arms around her waist and cradled her against his chest for a moment. He buried his face in her neck. She felt cherished. Loved. Protected. The warmth in his body seeped through to her heart for just a moment, a heartbeat of time she desperately needed to harden her resolve to protect him and his world. She pulled away. The birthmark over her heart was heating to boil-over, just like her nerves.

The heat radiating off his skin was strong, reassuring. His right hand captured hers and squeezed. While her gaze lingered on their joined fingers her brain tried to tell her heart not to get its hopes up for happily-ever-after. Her heart wasn't listening.

Silence stretched between them for so long she looked up at him out of sheer curiosity. He was staring at her. His eyes drowned her with a deadly combination of tenderness and raw animal lust. In vain, she searched for something to say. This was it. Showtime. Maybe they'd all live happily ever after, and maybe they'd all be dead in three weeks.

"Luke, I…" What could she say? Thanks for everything and I hope we both aren't dead tomorrow? When she opened her mouth, even she was surprised by the words that tumbled out. "Thanks for believing me."

"Sure." The man's smile could melt snow in January. "Promise me one thing."

"What?"

"No matter what happens tonight, you won't disappear on me."

No matter what happens…

That was a tall order.

"Alexa." His fingers caught her chin and forced her to meet his gaze. "Even if we only have three weeks, I want to spend every minute of it with you."

Tears rose, seared the back of her eyelids and collected on her eyelashes like dew on rose petals. "What if we succeed?"

Infinitely tender, his thumb caressed her bottom lip. "That's easy. I want forever."

Was he for real? Did he realize what he was offering her? A home here. A life. Love? He hadn't mentioned love. "You don't even know me."

"Oh, yes I do, angel. After sixteen years of dreams, you'd be surprised what I know."

He leaned over and kissed her. His lips were firm and gentle. Passionate and patient. The kiss was a promise. And a warning.

You'd be surprised…

Hell. The sexiest man she'd ever met was making her knees weak talking about forever. Could his timing be any worse? Here she was on a foreign world, facing an impossible task, listening for death's footsteps. In self-defense, her head fell back when his lips would have lingered, an entreaty to the heavens for help. She groaned. She wasn't sure she could handle any more surprises.

Luke nuzzled her neck. "Now, go. Snoop. Find the weasel and then come get back-up. That little case is almost indestructible. Let me help you. Don't you dare try to handle this by yourself."

She squeezed him once, hard, then let go. "I'll be fine."

His lips hovered next to her ear. "I don't care how much crap you're hiding under that skirt, none of it will save you if he opens that case. Be damn careful."

He knew she heard him, but wasn't that confident she was really listening. She disappeared right there in his arms. Petal soft lips brushed his with heat. Her touch lingered on his arm, then was gone. His heart skipped a beat, then resumed pounding a warning through his entire body. Alexa was going to do something crazy. He could feel it coming, inevitable, like the sun setting. Sixteen years ago, the man in white told him he would have to save her. Come hell or high water, he intended to do just that.

After a deep breath, he squared his shoulders, shook off the drugging effects of her lips, and reached into his jacket pocket to pull out his link to the invisible army surrounding them. With a flick of his wrist, the earpiece slid into place and he was instantly sucked into the Colonel's world. Alexa didn't know it, but the Colonel had a lot more than two men here. How the Colonel had pulled it off, Luke had no idea. But almost half the staff had been replaced with his people. Professionals. Killers. Experts. And every single one of them, from the parking garage to the kitchen, was on the look-out for Mr. Matthew Kline and the bug conceived with a pipette and a petri dish.

That left him free to follow his passion, and make sure she stayed out of trouble. The mark on his chest was a homing beacon. The Shen was cooling. She was getting too far away. Alexa Antwyr would hate to know that he could sense her presence, or lack of, through the strange matching mark on his chest. Eternity. Protection.

He smiled.

She was the flame.

He was the moth.

Time to dance.

* * *

Alexa had been to enough of these things with her father to know how the game was played. She could smile and make small talk with people she didn't know. Flirt. Lead anyone in a conversation to talk about themselves so they'd have nothing to say about her later. And she could conserve her energy until she really needed it. Already, she'd circuited the room twice and seen no sign of her prey. Neither the Colonel nor Kline were anywhere to be seen. Hunting two men made her feel like a femme fatale from a bad horror movie.

Why hide? According to the picture the Colonel's man had shown to Luke, Matthew Kline was young, in his twenties, and handsome in a boy-next-door kind of way. Maybe he had a thing for blonds?

No. That would be too easy.

She drifted closer to the dance floor and the grand piano in the recessed area behind it, an untouched champagne glass in her left hand. A tall, elegant woman in a blue sequined dress with dark skin and hair was singing about love and the blues. The Blues. Whatever the hell that was. Just wondering made her homesick.

But then there was Luke. He was here. In this world. Following her around the party. Did he think she was blind? Or perhaps he hoped his presence would keep her out of trouble. Hah! Just thinking about him made her smile. And made her want to stay.

Luke thought she didn’t know about all the Colonel’s men. He’d forgotten one important thing. The Colonel didn’t know she was involved. She’d been the one eavesdropping on all of the Colonel’s private conversations this afternoon. Not Luke. She was the one who knew who Matthew Kline really was and just how far the Colonel would go to protect him. Knew, and wished she didn’t.

Ω

Chapter Seven

The heavy red and gold carpeting muffled her footsteps. Brilliant city lights glowed outside the floor to ceiling wall of windows overlooking downtown. Many guests hovered near the windows to enjoy their view from the twenty-first floor. None of those people were of any interest to Alexa. They were in her way.

Auxiliary rooms beckoned to her from behind their closed doors. The one man she'd been determined to shadow this evening had managed to weave his way into the crowd and disappear. Luke was still following her around like a guard dog. She loved him for it, but she also knew she'd never catch her adversary if Luke's shadow was pacing hers all night. The mouse won't play until the cat's away.

Seizing an opportunity, she slid into one of the stalls in the ladies room, and vanished. A vivid image of Luke cursing outside the door in about five minutes forced her to suppress a giggle. When he realized she'd given him the slip he was not going to be happy. A small smile curved her lips. He was the first man to ever treat her like she was helpless. Her father and brothers had known better than to mess with her and her mother had made sure she had both the knowledge and the will to back it up. Still, his worry was endearing. Too bad she couldn't allow the poor man to keep that delusion. Being a pampered princess for the rest of her life didn't sound too bad. Especially, if Luke was going to be the one doing the spoiling.

Enough daydreaming. The Plaza Club had twelve private rooms and she'd only checked half of them.

She cracked the door open on another dark and empty room. The sign labeled this one The Colonel's Room. Fitting. Light from the main dining hall's chandeliers and wall sconces was enough for her to see that the room was empty. Her teeth bit down on her tongue to tame the curse struggling to fly from her lips. A mere three feet away stood a group of extremely old, incredibly wealthy women. Wouldn't do to give one of the old bats a heart attack. One of those obnoxiously large diamond rings they were all flinging around as they spoke would have to be handed down. Unless, of course, they requested to be buried with their jewelry. That wouldn't surprise her at all.

Stomach rumbling, she lifted a gourmet treat from an unattended waiter's tray and popped it into her mouth. At least she wouldn't starve. Seven rooms down, five to go. Methodical. Logical. Her father would be so proud. And it felt dead wrong.

She was thankful for the piano music and the noisy chatter all around her. Her gut instincts told her she could check rooms all night and she wouldn't find him. Time to stop looking for the weasel, and start thinking like one.

Where would she be if she wanted to infect everyone in this room? Who here had the most access to the most people? She stopped moving and just watched the natural rhythm of the room. The guests seated in heavy walnut chairs for dinner, chatting, laughing, showing off. The wait-staff, silently and efficiently keeping everything clean and everyone's glass full. Several couples were dancing to a slow, sad number the piano man and his mistress softly layered into the noise of the room.

The sight of all those couples dancing made her wish she was here just to enjoy the party like everyone else. She took a deep breath and straightened her shoulders. Duty demanded otherwise. Once Kline was stopped, she could dance with Luke every night if she wanted to. The thought of her lover made her birthmark flare to life. Great. Just what she needed right now. Distraction.

"Dance with me." Rock-solid arms slid around her waist and pulled her bare back against a wall of warmth.

Biting back a scream, Alexa realized Luke had found her. He pulled her around, his broad shoulders hid her from view of the party so she could reappear without scaring anyone. She released her hold on the light and scowled up at him. "How did you find me?"

Damn, but the man had a killer smile. Full of secrets. "Come on. Dance with me. There are thirty professional spies, sneaks, and assassins here. All looking for one little boy. Let them handle it, angel. Just for five minutes."

No woman in existence could have turned him down in that moment. Not with those sexy bedroom eyes devouring her like she was a special treat. She could see everything that happened in the room from the dance floor. Why not kill two birds with one stone? "All right. But just one dance."

He whirled her onto the floor and wrapped his arms around her like he was never going to let her go. A slow, sultry number was playing. Her body rocked against Luke's. His breath played over her neck when he dipped his head down to completely enclose her in their own private world. The soft fabric of his tuxedo rubbed against her cheek. The smell of his spicy shaving cream lingered on his skin. His lips dipped to brush her bare shoulder with a barely-there caress. He held her right hand in his, trapped between their bodies, right on top of the mark over his heart. It was hot.

Five minutes was hell when you wanted forever. But she'd take it. The world could wait.

Sighing, she closed her eyes and snuggled close enough to rub her forehead against his cheek like a purring cat. Contentment made her limbs weak and her eyelids heavy. What she wouldn't give to simply melt into him. Alexa never had been able to lie worth a damn. Especially to herself. She could pretend to be noble, pretend that she would try to save the world out of a sense of duty, honor, or moral fortitude. But in that moment, she admitted the truth to herself. Perhaps she'd wanted to save the world once. Now she was doing it for him. If that was a blight against her soul, so be it.

The song ended, but it took a moment for awareness to fight its way through the sensual haze of Luke's embrace. He loosened his hold and she slipped out of his arms.

Luke's thumb feathered over her cheek and he brushed a quick kiss over her lips. "In a few hours, I'll make sure you look at me like that for the rest of the night."

Quickly she looked away and hoped he wouldn't notice the heat she felt coloring her cheeks or the shiver that ran up her spine. Just because he noticed her reaction to him didn't mean he had to point it out. "What look?"

That damn smile again.

"Fine." Nope. Couldn't lie worth a damn. She leaned up on tiptoe and kissed him again because she had to. A quick, hard kiss that temporarily satisfied her new addiction to his taste. "Now, stop baby-sitting me and let me do my job."

With a sly wink and a last lingering touch on her shoulder he walked away.

What kind of response was that? He had every intention of dogging her footsteps for the rest of the night. Obviously, he had a hell of a lot more faith in all the Colonel's boys than she did. She needed air. And she needed a place where she could disappear again without drawing attention.

A quick search of the room confirmed what she already knew. It was either into the foyer to hide behind one of the archways, or back into the ladies room.

Darting in and out of view, a face caught her eye and the air froze in her chest. *Thank God.* She'd started to worry that the ringmaster wouldn't show up to run his own circus. But there he was. She'd been waiting two hours for the bastard to show himself again. Now she just had to keep him in her sights. No time to hide. If someone saw her disappear, they'd just have to write it off to too much champagne.

Two days of constant practice made bending the light second nature to her now. She disappeared instantly and darted across the room, dodging those she could, bumping into those she couldn't. The free flow of alcohol in the room was all the cover she was going to get. Judging by the dazed looks on the faces of the few she bumped into, it would be enough.

The service elevator doors were sliding closed when she caught up to him. She shoved her arm between the doors and gritted her teeth as the mechanical beasts bit into her arm, then slid back open. A huge, terrifying man with a shaved head, square jaw and a pockmarked face stood next to the panel. He was dressed all in black. His thick meaty hands looked like they could bend steel, or snap her in two. Pushing the button again he stared hard at his companion.

Great. She hadn't counted on the big guy. He probably outweighed her by a hundred pounds. Hell. There'd be no second chances with him. But there was no going back.

Alexa flowed into the corner, silent as the fog. She tried not to move, or breathe, as the doors closed and the big machine started to fall. The weight of her gun on her ankle was strangely comforting. Assuming she had time to reach for it.

As soon as the elevator was moving, the Colonel reached down to adjust something on his belt and then pulled an earpiece out of his left ear. "You got him?"

"Yes, sir." The big man's deep voice resonated in the confined space and made her feel like the bones of her skull could rattle right off her neck. Without question, he was the most frightening man she'd ever seen. The bastard had to be six-five, if he was an inch.

"Good. Does he have the virus with him?" The Colonel's left eyelid twitched a few inches from the big guy's shoulder.

"Yes, sir." Alexa wanted to cry with relief.

"No one else saw him?"

"No, sir. Caught him on the north service elevator."

Some of the starch seemed to leave the Colonel's shorts. Shoulders slumped in weariness beneath his tuxedo jacket, he ran a hand through his short gray hair with obvious relief. "I won't forget this, Patrick."

"I'm counting on it, sir." The Colonel reached into his jacket pocket and withdrew a heavy envelope. Alexa assumed it was full of cash. The envelope disappeared from view in the giant's hands. He handed the Colonel a small key in return.

Hah! Her instincts about the Colonel were right. They had him!

They had the virus! All she had to do was follow them straight to Matthew Kline and finish it. This was it. The end of the road. Her attention darted between the Colonel's aging face, lined with resignation, and the mammoth size body of the brute in black next to him.

She sent a silent prayer to the Lord thanking Him for the invention of gunpowder and bullets that evened her odds against the big brute, and to ask for a wee little bit of help. This was going to be one wild ride.

* * * * *

Luke felt her leave. The muscles in his back and neck clenched so tightly he thought they would explode. Damn her. Where the hell was she going?

To save the world.

"Shit." Hurrying to the elevators, he counted the seconds until the yawning entrance beckoned him to follow her. He darted in and pushed every single damn button on the panel. Twenty floors. There'd be no way to know which floor she was on until the door opened. Grateful for the link between them burned into his chest, he couldn't help wishing the old man had fine-tuned the damn thing a little better. All he could feel was her drifting farther away. His gut told him she was in over her head. Didn't need to be a rocket scientist to figure that one out.

He pulled his handgun from his ankle holster, made sure a bullet was in the chamber, and let the quiet dip of the elevator beneath his feet calm him. His little lady acted like she was indestructible. She was going to save the world. All right. Fine. He was going to help her whether she like it or not. Damn stubborn woman. The grudging respect he felt for her courage didn't ease the painful grip of the giant fist squeezing the hell out of his heart.

First stop. Twentieth floor. The doors slid silently open and he waited for the flash of heat her presence would bring to his chest. Silence. Darkness. Cold.

Nothing.

The doors slid closed and he clenched his teeth. One down,

nineteen to go. He willed the damn elevator to hurry. “Hang on, angel. I’m coming.”

Ω
Chapter Eight

The Colonel was breaking plenty of rules to protect Matthew Kline. He slinked through the dark hallways of the building like a snake with his private one-man army, while the rest of his team continued to search for Kline in ignorance. Taking out two men would be a hell of a lot easier than thirty, but history was working against her. This had all happened before. If Matthew Kline was trapped down here with daddy, how did the virus get to the party?

Something must go wrong with the Colonel's plan. She had to figure out what before it happened again. Maybe she should just shoot them all the first chance she got, grab the case, and run like the devil was chasing her. Her blood chilled to cold jelly in her veins. She didn't want to kill anyone. But she was afraid she wouldn't have a choice. The Colonel wasn't going to let her just waltz in there and bury a few bullets in his precious son.

The hair on her arms rose in alarm and a cold shiver raced over her skin like Death was introducing himself a little early. The Colonel was going to be a problem.

She followed the Colonel and Patrick as quickly as her soft leather slippers allowed. The floor was full of deserted offices. A few scattered lights provided minimal illumination, which suited her just fine. Less light meant she'd need less energy to control it. The shadows were on her side.

"Who's he?" Anger laced the Colonel's words when he saw another man in black standing guard in front of a closed office door. He was smaller than Patrick, dark skin and hair. Thin, wiry frame and face. Utter and absolute blankness stared out from behind his dark eyes. No conscience. No soul. Even more terrifying than Patrick. The devil incarnate handed the Colonel a set of keys, but didn't deign to answer.

"He's with me." Alexa figured Patrick wasn't willing to argue about it. The Colonel must have thought the same. Hell. Three of them now. Plus Kline. Luck wasn't playing fair.

"Wait by the elevators and make sure none of my boys spot you."

"Yes, sir."

Alexa held her breath as Brute and Brute Jr. passed within two feet of her and kept walking around the corner. The scary men in black were gone. Well, gone enough. She could find the stairs. Luck was playing nice after all.

The Colonel stood alone in the hallway, his head slumped, his entire focus on the keys jingling in his hand. He looked sad. Tired. Worn to the bone by life.

If he hadn't been a schemer and a liar, if he hadn't been responsible for the annihilation of an entire planet, she might have felt sorry for him. Instead, she reached for her gun with her right hand and one of her knives with her left. She'd try to avoid killing them. The only thing she needed was the little silver case. The Colonel and his personal problems wouldn't kill the world. But a mere fifty feet stood between her and a life of happily-ever-after with Luke. She'd be damned if she'd get this close and fail.

The Colonel opened the door and walked into the room, and out of sight. Sprinting for the large door, which was slowly swinging closed, she managed to wedge it open a couple of inches with her foot. She should be able to slide into the room unnoticed. Unless the latch clicked when the door closed. Then she would have a problem.

Shimmying sideways through as small an opening as possible she let the door slide home behind her.

Matthew Kline sat, both wrists handcuffed to his sides in a large leather-backed chair. His jeans and T-shirt were wrinkled and stained. Long brown hair hung, greasy and limp, to his shoulders. Hazel eyes spit hatred at the old man slumped in the chair across from him. And there, in the center of an otherwise bare desktop, sat the silver case.

"What am I going to do with you, boy?"

Matthew struggled in vain against the handcuffs. "Let me go."

"Do you know how much trouble you've caused? This isn't like picking pockets or stealing cars! You're carrying around deadly pathogens that were stolen from a Four Lab." The Colonel leaned forward, his elbows resting on his knees. "Killing Trent was stupid, son. Taking the virus was worse. Every senator on committee is breathing fire down my neck. Those boys don't screw around. I don't think I can protect you this time."

"Go to hell. I never asked for your help. Just leave me the fuck alone."

"What are you doing here? How the hell did you get near Trent?"

Insanity blazed like deadly laser beams from Matthew's eyes. Alexa was glad he couldn't see her. "Everyone has a price."

'Damn it, Matt."

"You can't lock people up, play God with their lives. You think you're so much better than me." The handcuffs jerked and strained as Matthew renewed his struggle against the arms of the chair. "The whole fucking world wants to lock me away and forget I exist."

"How'd you get out? Why wasn't I notified?" An evil sneer crossed Matthew's face in response. Alexa inched closer to the desk, the bug. This kid was nuts.

"Mom signed me out."

"That bitch." Alexa barely heard the whispered curse, but Matthew shifted forward and threw his weight onto his feet. The chair, still strapped to him, rose off the floor until the chair legs stuck out. He stood like a man who bore the weight of the world on his back, and was losing his footing. Spittle sprayed the desktop with every hoarse word Matthew shouted.

"You'd leave me locked in that fucking hospital forever. Mom never should've married you. You're not my father!"

The Colonel's shaking hand wrapped around the raised black handle of the silver case. "Not anymore."

Screaming his rage, Matthew bent forward until he lifted the chair legs above desk level. He swung his whole body around to strike his father with the base. A black wheel struck the Colonel's hand and the silver case flew. It skidded to a stop on the floor against the far wall of the office with a thunk. The wall farthest from Alexa.

The Colonel raged around the corner of the desk to stop his son. His shoulder slammed into her head. She staggered back in a daze. It hurt like hell.

"What the…"

Alexa darted out from beneath his arms just as Matthew swung around in another manic circle, striking out at his father with the chair. He missed. The Colonel was almost on him. Matthew rammed head first, straight into the Colonel's chest and toppled him to the ground.

Dropping her dagger, she wrapped her hand around the small case handle like a drowning woman holding onto a lifejacket. Time to leave this wonderful family love fest behind.

She ran for the door and pulled it open. Patrick blocked her exit. The noise must've alerted him. Without a word Patrick shoved her out of his way and barreled into the room. He yanked Matthew, chair and all, off his father. The Colonel thanked him as she ran for the elevators. Then, "Where's the case?"

"The woman took it, sir." Oh, God. He'd seen her. She must have dropped her guard in her panic. Fear pushed her legs to move faster. Her mind was in utter chaos. She couldn't focus her thoughts enough to bend the light again. They could see her!

"What woman?" The Colonel's voice filled the hallway. "Shit. Move! Move!"

Alexa glanced back over her shoulder in time to see the Colonel's gun pointed at her. Cradling the deadly case of M-6 to her stomach, she wrapped her left forearm over it like armour. She could die, but the case had to survive. Intact.

Two bullets whizzed by her head. The Colonel yelled at her. "Stop! Don't make me shoot you."

Not a chance in hell she was letting this case out of her hands. She dashed around the corner toward the elevators with the men hot on her heels. Her birthmark blazed on her chest, a reminder of her destiny. She kept running.

"Damn it." The Colonel's words reached her a second before his third shot seared her left shoulder. Pain sent her staggering against the wall but she held onto the case. Only death would pry it from her fingers now. She reached over blindly and pushed the call button with the butt of her gun, then wrapped her right arm protectively around her cargo. Blood dripped down from her left shoulder, smeared the outside of the silver case, tarnished its perfection.

How fitting. Little killer bugs. Blood for blood.

Patrick stalked toward her. Turning, she leaned her right shoulder against the wall between the two elevators for support. She needed Patrick in her sights. Gun raised, the solid wall was all that kept her aim steady, pointed right at him. He stopped. For now. His gaze darted farther down the hallway, then settled on her face. "Come on, bitch. That's not playing nice."

The devil gave her no warning, just shoved the barrel of a gun against the base of her skull. "Drop it." Patrick's partner sounded like he could be could yawn as easily as blow her head off.

Spots swam before her eyes and her ears were ringing. She held onto the gun for all she was worth. "I don't care about any of this. Just let me go."

"Can't do that, my dear. You have stolen property and I need to take it back." The Colonel stopped when he reached Patrick's side. They were about twenty feet away. She was caught like a fish who'd already swallowed the hook. The Colonel held out his hand. "Give me the case."

Her skirt was stained red from the steadily running blood. She swayed, then caught herself. The jerk with the gun didn't shoot her, but no one was coming to save her. No one knew where she was. Luke was right. Some help would be nice. Too bad he wasn't here to gloat over it.

The elevator dinged. Her ride was here. Time to save herself.

Or die.

Funny how staring death in the face could clear a girl's head.

Swaying forward like she was going to faint, she let her arms fall limply to her sides. With a flick of her wrist, she tossed the case toward the opening elevator doors. Relief flooded her when the bugs landed just inside the doors.

Halfway to the ground she disappeared. She hit hard and rolled onto her back. Her foot connected with the gunman's left knee, buckling his leg. He fell away from her into the hallway with a curse.

As fast as she could, she pulled herself forward on her elbows. Every movement jarred her shoulder, shattered her focus so they could see her. Crawl faster! *Damn this dress.* Legs tangled in the soft folds, for once she actually hated the feminine vanity that now trapped her. Her shoulders just cleared the doors when the weasel's hand shackled her ankle and pulled her arms out from under her. She landed on her injured shoulder and cried out in pain. Rolling onto her side, she kicked her attacker. Patrick barreled toward her in a dead run.

A gunshot rang out. Patrick staggered forward dragging one leg. Another shot tore into his opposite hip. He crashed into the unforgiving floor, chest heaving for air.

Half of Luke's torso darted out from inside the elevator. He shot the man holding her ankle. She didn't bother looking back to see if he was dead. Rolling into the elevator, she curled into a protective ball around the case of M-6.

"Stay down." Luke crouched beside her. Matthew ran toward them from farther down the hall. Rage etched deep lines in his face. He held the Colonel's keys in one hand, and Alexa's abandoned knife in the other. Luke's gun held the Colonel pinned in place. The old man dropped to one knee and reached for his weapon. Luke fired. The doors slid closed, erasing the Colonel's stunned face, the hole in his forehead, from her vision. The elevator lurched to life beneath her as Matthew's scream penetrated the thick elevator doors. The Colonel was dead.

"Luke..."

"Just shut-up and don't move, or I'll shoot you myself."

She laughed. It hurt. "I love you."

He shook his head. "Just shut-up, Alexa." His jacket hit the floor. The elevator doors opened, then closed. They were moving again. He ripped one white sleeve from his arm and tied the material around her bleeding shoulder. "If you ever scare me like that again..."

Apparently, he couldn't finish the thought. His words were rough, but his hands were gentle as he helped her sit up and lean back against the elevator's wall. She stopped trying to talk and just let relief wash over her. They were alive. They had the virus. And as soon as they could get back to the lab, M-6 would be wiped off the face of the Earth.

Luke spoke into a microphone wrapped around his watchband. "Eleventh floor, Sean. Two mercs and the Colonel shot. Kline's there, too."

Alexa could almost feel the collective force of movement in the building as the complete focus of thirty armed men and women shifted to the eleventh floor. Luke listened, then shook his head. "I'll explain later. Just get down there."

Stop. Doors open. Closed. Her stomach lurched when they started moving again. "Who's Sean?"

"A friend."

Silence. Stop. Doors slid open. Doors slid closed. "Where are we going?"

"I had to push every damn button to try and find you." His fingertips caressed the hair that had come loose around her face, then tucked the stray strands behind her ear. "Ten floors." A shudder passed through him. "You're lucky it wasn't eleven. I wouldn't've made it in time."

"How did you find me?"

With shaking fingers he pulled her hand to rest against the mark on his chest. Her mind calmed. The pull between her heart and his, the binding force, stole her breath for a moment. Talk about being branded. “Thanks.”

“Anytime.” The doors slid open behind Luke. He pulled her to her feet and stepped out onto the main floor. “Come on, angel. Let’s get out of here.”

“How sweet.” Matthew Kline was waiting for them, panting from his sprint down the stairwell. “I’ll take that.” He wrenched the case from Alexa’s hand. The gun he held to Luke’s head made sure neither of them protested. Matt’s maniacal gaze rested on her for a moment, then dismissed her as unimportant. “You can go.”

Wrenching Luke’s arm behind his back with a jerk he shoved him back into the elevator. “You’re going upstairs with me. We’re going to finish this.”

No time to think. Luke watched her raise her skirt. Acceptance flashed in his eyes. He was giving her permission to miss. It made her love him more.

“Matthew!” Alexa’s challenge rang through the air.

Matthew Kline looked up an instant before her knife buried itself in his eye socket. Never mess with a woman who knows how to throw knives.

Luke stepped away and let him fall.

Alexa threw herself in his arms. Cheek nestled against the heated mark on his chest, she breathed him in. His head rested on top of hers. Comforting hands gently slid up and down her back. “Damn it, woman. What am I going to do with you?”

She smiled in answer, “Take me to bed for a solid week and ravish me at your leisure?”

“For starters.” His lips devoured hers. Every bit of adrenaline running rampant in their systems was redirected into the heat of that kiss. When he lifted his head, neither one of them could breathe. “I love you, angel.”

She stared into his eyes. He stared back. Forever was looking pretty damn good.

Ω
Chapter Nine

"How do you know?" Luke was lying on his side. He nuzzled her bare breast and decided that a week wasn't nearly long enough to keep her in bed. With his free hand, he caressed her abdomen, stared at her skin in wonder. "Are you sure?"

"I'm sure." Alexa smiled and ran her fingers through his hair.

"But how do you know?" *A daughter.* A baby girl who would steal his heart and wrap him around her tiny finger the first moment he saw her.

His wife's gentle laugh was full of feminine secrets. "I'm all-powerful and all-knowing."

"I'll show you 'all-powerful'." Luke rolled on top of her, pinning her to the soft green sheets beneath them. A full moon illuminated her naked body and perfect skin through the large bay windows of his bedroom. Her eyes were unreadable, their expression lost in the darkness of the room. She looked mysterious and sexy as hell. Her hair spread around her like a halo of liquid silver. Like an angel. *His angel.*

Like a moth to a flame, his tongue traced a path over her skin to the Shen above her breast. He traced the heated circle, savoring the taste of her flesh, the answering burn of his own mark as hers flared to life. She arched her back, thrust her nipples into the air, begging for attention, driving him on. Her smooth legs spread beneath him, then lifted to wrap around his thighs so his hips dropped into the cradle of hers, the tip of his cock pressed into her slick wet heat. She was more than ready for him.

The knowledge forced a groan from him. He sucked her nipple into his mouth, flicked the tip with his tongue, then sucked hard, fast, with a rhythm he'd learned would drive her crazy. She writhed, tried to lift her hips off the bed to take all of him.

He wanted to go slowly, to worship her, to thank her for the miracle now growing inside her body. But the wet heat pulling at him drove every sane thought from his mind. With one hard thrust he surged into her. A shocked cry of welcome fell from her lips and Alexa opened for him, pulled him deeper. She was incredibly hot, tight. Her muscles clenched around him in both demand and invitation. He tightened his stomach muscles and pressed hard, rubbing against her most sensitive spot as he thrust and withdrew, steadily increasing the pace.

Luke sought her lips with his. Of their own accord, his hands sought hers and held them entwined on either side of her head. The heat of her mouth beckoned. He thrust his tongue inside, mated with hers, plunging deep in unison with the forceful driving of his hips. The Shen burned on his chest as if it were on fire, spreading the flames to every millimeter of skin that rubbed against hers.

Luke let go of her arms and pulled back to take in the sight of her writhing beneath him in passion. He would be lost for all time in the pleasure of her body, the fierceness of her spirit. The words poured from his heart, from his very soul. "I love you, Alexa."

She froze beneath him, then her smile melted him on the spot. "I love you, too."

Her hands wandered up his chest, pulled on his nipples. The touch jolted his senses, shot through his body. She pushed her pelvis against his, took him even deeper. Slowly, her tongue caressed her lower lip. It was a deliberate enticement, and he was beyond resisting, didn't want to fight the inferno rising to take them.

With a growl, he lowered his head to hers, plundered the sweetness of her mouth. He intended to hold something back, to protect the new life stirring inside her womb, but her soft voice demanded he push harder, begged him until he wanted nothing more than to bury his body so deeply into hers that she'd never get him out.

Alexa met every thrust with one of her own. Her tongue dueled with his for supremacy, staking *her* claim. She cried out her release and he followed her over the edge into bliss.

When they recovered, he pulled her to his side, her head resting in the nook of his shoulder. Her hands traced devilish patterns of desire onto his chest, tempting him to rise again.

He clamped his hand over hers to stop the sweet torment. “How do you know, Alexa?”

Sexy, delicate shoulders lifted in a little shrug. “I can’t explain it. I just know.”

“And you’re sure it’s a girl?”

“Yes.”

A daughter with blue eyes and silver hair. Beautiful. Luke drifted off to sleep with a smile on his face.

* * *

White fog wrapped around Luke in welcome. He was dreaming again.

The Archiver beckoned. The ageless one. The man in white. The man with secrets. The man who made promises...and kept them.

What? He wanted to shout until his voice was hoarse, but he knew the man never answered questions. Luke would see only what he was meant to. Maybe the Archiver needed reassurance, was worried about Alexa. “She’s safe. M-6 was destroyed. I’ll take care of her. You know I will.”

The man nodded. Smiled. Was that a twinkle in his eye?

Luke followed along after him in the blank white space that he was, after sixteen years, well accustomed to. Then the old man waved his hand and a vision sprang to life before them.

She was about three years old. Bouncing red curls framed a pixie face dusted with freckles and blue eyes the exact shade of her mother’s. His little girl was running in the grass wearing a bright yellow sundress and sandals. On her ankle, like a shackle, was the Shen, the Mark of the Taken. Alexa ran after her. Caught her. Swung her, laughing, into the air.

Luke froze, sure his heart was going to explode. Once again he stood and bravely faced his future, instantly fell in love with someone he had yet to meet, someone he'd die to protect. His little girl….

Tired eyes lined with fine wrinkles focused on Luke's face with demand, and respect. For the second time in sixteen years he spoke. "Your daughter. Guard her well. She is needed."

Join my New Release Alerts e-mail list @
http:www.michelecallahan.com
(Just New Release E-mails…Nothing Else)

Books by Michele Callahan

Timewalker Chronicles:
RED NIGHT
SILVER STORM
BLUE ABYSS (May 2014)
BLACK GATE (June 2014)
WHITE FIRE (June 2014)

The Chimera Series:
CHIMERA BORN (June 2014)
Coming Soon – Chimera's Kiss

The Ozera Wars:
ROGUE'S DESTINY
QUEEN'S DESTINY
WARRIOR'S DESTINY
Coming Soon – Hunter's Destiny

Red Night: Published by Michele Callahan
http://www.michelecallahan.com
http://romcon.com

About The Author:

Michele Callahan is a wife, mother, romance and science fiction addict, and founder of RomCon, the only Fan Convention geared toward women who read romance and genre fiction. Suffering from a healthy case of sci-fi/fantasy fever, Michele never turns down an opportunity to sit through a Star Wars, True Blood, or Matrix marathon.

Her favorite things in books; hot heroes, superpowers, freakish things that can't be explained by modern science, and true love! Her past jobs include fast-food drive through goddess, nurse's aide, cashier, anatomy & physiology instructor, medical office nurse, and entrepreneur. When she's at home her life is ruled by her family plus two 100 pound rescue dogs and their wagging tails (which should really be classified as dangerous weapons.)

Her all-time favorite movie list includes: The Matrix, Terminator, Star Wars - The Empire Strikes Back, The Princess Bride, and Jerry Maguire. (BTW- She doesn't understand that list either…)

Timewalker Chronicles, Book 2:

SILVER STORM

by Michele Callahan

TIMEWALKER CHRONICLES BOOK 1: RED NIGHT

SILVER STORM

Lost…

On a hot summer night twenty-five years ago a freak lightning bolt struck Sarah St. Pierre on Lake Michigan. Presumed dead, her body was never found. She simply…vanished.

Hunted…

Timothy Daniel Tucker retired, but the group of people he once worked for aren't willing to give him up so easily. They watch him, waiting for him to crack, waiting for an excuse to bring him back in to finish what he started.

When Tim finds a beautiful naked woman floating in Hendrick's Lake, he suspects a trap. She claims to be the same woman who disappeared over two decades ago, but she hasn't aged a day. Worse, she knows intimate details about his covert work on a weapon that could destroy all of humanity. Trust is impossible, but Tim will not stop until he discovers all of her secrets, until he uncovers the truth.

Hunted by an unseen enemy, Sarah claims to see things no one else can see, to know things about the future that no one could possibly know. And she has a frightening power no human should wield. Falling in love is an unacceptable risk but Tim can't walk away from her visions, her power, or the fierce desire she ignites within him. Predator or prey? Truth or lies? Love or duty? Decisions must be made. Millions of lives hang in the balance…

…and the clock is ticking.

Silver Storm: Chapter One

Friday, 5:17 AM

Glowing silver embers fell from the sky over Chicago and all of her suburbs. The glittering snowflakes spread over the city faster than dawn could shoot its rays of new morning light. Night hung on by her fingernails, the sun trapped behind the horizon for a precious few minutes. The early risers, those who initially believed themselves blessed to witness a miracle, gasped in awe and cried at the unearthly beauty floating down over them like a billion falling stars.

Then the screaming began as everything and everyone, nine million people, burned to ash in a matter of minutes.

Three Days Earlier, 5:17 AM

Silence hovered over the water and a few moments of peace settled over Tim like a cool mist on a hot July day. He grinned and finished tying the spinner on his line. The soft lapping sounds against the side of his aluminum boat, smell of wet vegetation, and honking geese gliding around the edges of Hendrick Lake were as far from the deserted lab, blazing heat and gunfire as he could get. Tuesday morning meant most people were back at work, leaving the lake and the best fishing spots empty…just the way he liked it.

Bandit curled up in her bed on the floor of the nine-foot boat, content to sleep for a few more hours. The tiny Pekingese mix was used to Tim's routine. Fish. Run. Scan the news headlines every night for things he dreaded to see.

He'd sit at the computer and she'd curl up in his lap. She did everything with him now. When he'd flown home to bury his parents, she'd been a four-month old puppy he could fit inside his combat boot. He'd come home on six months mandatory leave to *'get his head back in the game.'* The top brass didn't like the fact that his research was turning up nothing but rotten eggs. Nothing was said, but it didn't take a rocket scientist to know they hoped the death of his parents would push him deeper into the game. He had nothing left now but a dog, an empty house and scars. Lots of scars.

Bandit hopped up and yipped at him, happily wagging her tail as if to remind him that he had *her*. And how dare he think he needed anything else? The princess of a puppy had been his mother's whim and a completely spoiled lap dog. The tiny pooch had lived a life of luxury traveling in his mother's purse everywhere she went. He'd considered giving the pup away after the funeral, but couldn't bring himself to do it. That was four months ago. The little girl wasn't much bigger now, a whopping ten pounds soaking wet, but she kept him company, she was smart, she liked to fish, and she was the only family he had left.

"Okay, fur ball. Let's see what we can catch today." Tim cast his line out over his favorite fishing spot and let the spinner sink a few inches before slowly reeling it back in. The rhythm and monotony chased away the last of his lingering nightmares.

Bandit growled low in her throat and paced over her pillow, rumbling like a tiny electric toy stuck in the 'On' position. The hair on her body started to rise, forming a round fluffy brown and white snowball with huge brown eyes. Bandit looked like a cartoon character. Tim would've laughed, but the hair on his arms crackled with static electricity as well and rose to attention like a thousand miniature soldiers. The water puckered as if it were being hit by raindrops, but there were no clouds. No rain. No thunderstorms on the horizon waiting to zap him and his boat into oblivion with a stray bolt of lightning.

Tim reeled in his line and stashed the fishing pole in its spot along the side of his seat. Bandit stood at rigid attention on her fluffy brown bed and continued to growl, a steady little rumble of warning that set his teeth on edge. They were too exposed on the water, too out in the open. He clenched his jaw to keep a stream of expletives from rolling off his tongue.

Perhaps this was a freak storm. There had to be a perfectly good explanation, because if it were the boys from the lab, he'd be dead already. No, whatever this was, it wasn't normal. His silence came as automatic as breathing. He didn't start the small trolling motor. He took out a wooden oar and paddled smoothly for the tree line behind his house. Two minutes, perhaps three, and he'd be under cover. He hoped that wouldn't be two minutes too long.

"Shit."

The electrical buzz building in the air continued to grow stronger until he could hear the slight hum around him. His skin prickled and the water on the side of the boat rose, forming hundreds of fluid stalagmites rising, bursting, and sinking back into the water faster than he could track them.

Earthquake? E.M.P? Geomagnetics? Had those bastards finally done it?

The electric charge shocked him with static build-up every time he moved. Time to get off the water before whatever was happening cooked him in place or worse.

He glided into the reeds only a few feet from shore and

tried to figure out how he could get off the boat without touching the supercharged water. Any second now he expected stunned or dead fish to start popping to the surface. Maybe the Fish and Game boys were doing this for a count or culling of the lake. He couldn't imagine why they would, but they should've posted warnings.

Bandit yelped and sunk to her belly, whimpering and shivering. A thunderous boom filled the air and a burst of silver light to his right blinded him. Instinct drove him to the bottom of his boat for cover. He grabbed Bandit and held her squirming torso down as his mind raced with possibilities.

A bomb? Lightning?

Whatever it was ruined a perfectly good fishing trip.

As suddenly as it all began, it was over. The supercharged air dissipated like it had never been and the hair on his arms returned to its usual resting place. His clothes stopped crackling. The water, roiling moments ago, returned to a serene and placid lapping against the side of his small boat. The geese took up their honking as if nothing out of the ordinary had just happened. Bandit suddenly leaped to her feet and jumped onto the bench seat he'd just vacated. Her curled tail wagged fiercely as she yapped at something just out of his sight.

Ears still ringing from the blast of lightning, he pulled his ever-present knife from its sheath at his waist and lifted his head just enough to see over the edge of the boat.

She floated face up at the water's edge. Unconscious. Naked. Her head was toward shore in no more than three or four inches of water, leaving the rest of her long, willowy body drifting alongside his boat. Was she dead? That's all he needed. Dead body, 9-1-1 call, and fifteen hours at the police station saying, 'I don't know,' until his tongue was bleeding.

Hell. He didn't dare get in the water and risk immediate electrocution. Bandit had no such inhibitions.

"No!"

Too late. The little wet rat swam happily to the woman's side and sniffed her hair, sopping wet tail wagging like a curled mop waving him into the water.

"You little turkey." With a sigh, he threw the small anchor and then jumped over the side after his crazy dog. He landed in knee-deep water and leaned over the woman, feeling for a pulse. His shoulders relaxed when the steady beat of her heart thrummed beneath his fingertips. Her chest rose and fell, her small, perfect breasts capturing his gaze as they followed the peaceful rhythm of a deep, dreamless sleep. No blood. No lacerations. No bumps on the head or obvious injury. She was, in a word, perfect.

Sun-bleached brown hair floated around her pale face in a halo of dark silk. Full, deep pink lips and dark lashes outlined her features like an artist's brush strokes. A light dusting of freckles gave her a pixie-like quality he found shockingly appealing. She looked like a sun-drenched California beach beauty, complete with tan lines from a itsy-bitsy bikini and a siren's hair. Long hair. Long everything. He guessed she was at least six feet tall, with incredibly long legs, a slender waist, and small tight breasts that would fit his hand to perfection. She was lean, like a gazelle, muscular and slim. Obviously either an athlete or someone obsessed with the gym.

What the hell was she doing naked, floating in a lake where she'd appeared from nowhere like a bad magic trick?

Her eyelids fluttered open to reveal dazed hazel green irises that seemed unable to focus on his face. Her whispered words shocked him.

"Timothy Daniel Tucker."

Three words. His name.

His whole name.

No one had called him that since his mother had thrown it around the house when he would behave like only a particularly aggravating teenage boy could. He was damn good at aggravating a woman when he wanted to be. At least when they were conscious....

Who are the Archivers? Why are they here?
And who are they fighting?
Find out in SILVER STORM – Available Now!

28309901R00059

Made in the USA
Charleston, SC
06 April 2014